THUG LIFE 2

Lock Down Publications and Ca$h Presents

Thug Life 2

A Novel by *Trai'Quan*

Lock Down Publications

P.O. Box 944
Stockbridge, Ga 30281

Lock Down Publications
Like our page on Facebook: Lock Down Publications @
www.facebook.com/lockdownpublications.ldp
Cover design and layout by: **Dynasty Cover Me**
Book interior design by: **Shawn Walker**
Edited by: **Lashonda Johnson**

Stay Connected with Us!

Text **LOCKDOWN** to 22828 to stay up-to-date with
new releases, sneak peaks, contests and more…
Thank you!

Submission Guideline.

Submit the first three chapters of your completed manuscript to ldpsubmissions@gmail.com, subject line: Your book's title. The manuscript must be in a .doc file and sent as an attachment. Document should be in Times New Roman, double spaced and in size 12 font. Also, provide your synopsis and full contact information. If sending multiple submissions, they must each be in a separate email.

Have a story but no way to send it electronically? You can still submit to LDP/Ca$h Presents. Send in the first three chapters, written or typed, of your completed manuscript to:

LDP: Submissions Dept
P.O. Box 944
Stockbridge, Ga 30281

DO NOT send original manuscript. Must be a duplicate.

Provide your synopsis and a cover letter containing your full contact information.

Thanks for considering LDP and Ca$h Presents.

When you visit the zoo, people usually tell you you're not allowed to feed the animals. You're not even allowed to pet some of them. Because to the animals that are not completely domesticated, you can actually be seen as food and the animals may just decide they're hungry. Probably at the same time you decide to be stupid!

"Crack done tore apart my family tree. My mother's on the shit, my father's tripping blaming me. Is it my fault cause I'ma young black male? Cops sweatin' me as if my destiny is making crack sales. Only fifteen and got problems. Cops on my ass, so I bail till I dodge 'em. They finally pull me over at the path, remember Rodney King, so I blast on they punk ass—"

Tupac's Soldiers Story!

How It All Began

It all started in Brooklyn N.Y. when he was just three-years-old, his mother moved them up North. As far as he knew she had been trying to escape one reality only to run into another one. The Brownsville housing was looked upon as one of the toughest neighborhoods in Brooklyn N.Y. Some people even referred to it as the jungle. The rapper *Old Dirty Bastard* once called all of Brooklyn the *Zoo*.

It was Brownville that was the concrete jungle. Nearly everybody in Brownsville was an animal. They all exhibited the unique character and personalities of various types of animals. Panthers, Pythons, Bears, Silverback gorillas, you name it. In Brownsville, someone had those same characteristics.

By birth, his given name had been Casey Porter. As a little nigga in a large jungle, he had to learn how to fend for himself at a young age.

They weren't rich or wealthy, but for some time he could say that his moms always did the best she could. Then too— there were those times when *good just wasn't good enough*. She'd fallen weak and started to get high. One drug led to another until she eventually came to the one that changed New York City. Heroin!

He really wasn't able to see it until he grew older. When he was thirteen, he began to understand just what was going on. Yet, there was nothing he could do to save her from the demons. So, all he could do was watch as her life withered away. Just before his 15th birthday, she overdosed, leaving him as a product of the homeless. He lived in their apartment by himself, the housing people were unaware, but the other animals knew. They even began calling him *Young* or *Young*

Cas. Because by this time he'd fully become one of the aggressive animals in the streets. *The Jungle!*

He'd never known who his old man was. His moms never talked about him. Except for that one time when she was too high to remember. She'd said something about some nigga beating on her while she was pregnant. He would never forget her saying that.

He never really knew what he wanted to be when he grew up. In his eyes, all life was fucked up. The animals were either husting, shooting dope, or smoking it. Or they were gang banging. Some were trying to find righteousness. A few were trying to do it all. When he came in contact with it, he didn't know what he was going to be, but he did know one thing. Whatever it was, being broke wasn't part of the deal. His dreams were bigger than that. Although none of the other animals wanted to give him a chance to get on his feet. They all heard him stressing about one day his chance would come. How on that day—at that time, *Young Castro* would be the future!

"In the jungle, you know we rumble with the beast, ain't nothing sweet, we got to eat—"

Son of Man 'Concrete Jungle'

Trai'Quan

Chapter One

"Aaahhh—God, please! Please help me!" The man screamed because of the excruciating pain he was experiencing.

He was tied face forward to the back of a chair, naked. His back was covered with welts, the blood had mixed with the sweat, so it was unable to dry up fast. In a way, it seemed to be pouring out of his body. Behind the man, standing with his shirt drenched in his own sweat, holding the whip in his left hand, and looking like he'd once owned an entire plantation of slaves was Poe. He wiped the sweat from his forehead and looked. He glanced over to where the other two men sat. They were all inside an abandoned warehouse across from the Bethlehem Community Center.

It used to be some type of cotton factory. Young Castro sat calmly and predatorily quiet as he smoked the Newport cigarette hanging from the corner of his mouth. Jeeta held his cellphone in hand texting and seemingly arguing with himself. Whatever that was about Poe couldn't say, and he wasn't about to get into anybody's business. Or personal one on one conversation.

Instead, he remembered that he had a job to do. Poe drew the whip back and lashed out again. The whip he used was a traditional cat-o-nine-tails that was made from a thick animal hide. Poe drew it back and flicked it as if he was the animal.

"Lord—have mercy—" the man's head came up as he cried out.

At one point in time, he'd also been an animal in the zoo. Inside, it was bothering Poe. He'd known this man since their earlier years in New York. Hustling, running the streets, and barking at the moon when they were young thugs. Poe shook his head because it didn't make any sense. When Young Castro first said that he needed them to come down here to

Augusta, GA to help him. They'd agreed then that they would all stick together. Bonded by the essence of New York Cities' upbringing. That nothing would be able to come between them. Poe watched as the new cut he made in Dawg's flesh began to bleed. It made him feel some kinda way.

"Young—please, please just go ahead and kill me—" Dawg pleaded.

When Poe looked over at Young Castro all he saw was Young lighting another Newport off the one that had gotten short, chain-smoking, which he'd been doing since they snatched Dawg up. Even he was wondering why Young Castro didn't just go ahead and kill the nigga.

Fraternizing with the enemy, Young Castro thought. *That's how disloyalty usually starts.*

In the streets, disloyalty was an unforgivable sin. It ranked up there alongside snitching and stealing. These were things any individual that was bred by the streets knew. Especially those bred in the jungle. If you were a bear, you hung with bears. If you were a wolf, you ran with wolves and lions roared with lions. It wasn't something you had to be told. The animals simply knew.

In the jungle, sympathy was for the weak. While compassion was for females and the young. Only justice existed for grown men who did things they weren't supposed to do and justice had no emotions. The bitch had a cover over her eyes and was colder than the morning breeze coming off the Hudson River. She wasn't looking at who did what crime. All she heard were the charges read off the indictment.

Young looked over to where Poe unleashed another blow from the whip. None of it affected him in any type of emotional way. He felt like he didn't have any emotions. Dawg cried out again and Young took another drag off the cigarette. He took in the smoke and felt it deep within his lungs. He still felt like an animal.

$$$$

"Stupid ass girl," Jeeta mumbled as he read the text that Crystal had just sent.

He looked up from time to time when he heard Poe's whip holding a conversation with flesh. How this nigga Dawg could bear it, he didn't know.

"Stupid muthafucka," he mumbled. How you gon' steal from the muthafucka that fed you? He never would have thought that Dawg, nor anyone in Young's crew would be shiesty. Then too, the way that Young explained it to him made sense.

Young Castro told him, *"Envy was an emotion that one person directed toward another. Without the other person, envy couldn't exist."* He'd said, *"Envy produces tragedies, and these tragedies occur everywhere in the world. Envy governs a lot of behaviors that exist between whites and blacks. Whites induced it into blacks during slavery. And it's been eating blacks up ever since."*

Jeeta had an open ear for things like slavery and black history. His great grandmother used to explain those things to him before she passed.

Young said, *"Envy, in no way can be a characteristic trait on which one can build brotherhood. That's why most organizations fall apart."*

Young explained that once an individual opens the door for envy to come into their hearts. The hate and lust would be close behind. Only to have greed follow and this Jeeta suspected was what went on with Dawg and they hadn't seen it.

When Raine first mentioned that she thought she'd seen Dawg riding around with someone in a gold Lexus GS. They hadn't thought much about it. Then a few weeks later Jeeta found out who drove the Lexus.

When Young first gave him the position of captain in his crew. Jeeta hadn't realized what that actually meant. Until he went with Young to pick up that first shipment. Jeeta saw right then and there that Young was no longer playing softball. He had stepped into the major league. Both Cream and Dawg were released because the federal witness they needed was dead, which meant the federal district attorney couldn't bring a successful case to trial. Of all those arrested, seventy of them walked, including Juggernot and Ace. Then Poe came home. The police were still looking for the two men who shot up the waffle house. Two off duty officers were shot there the same night.

While the GBI had the pressure down and all those people in jail. Young had been waiting for whatever he had in the makings. In between all this, two new dope dealers stepped up. Both were originally from Texas, they'd been in Augusta for some time now. Hustling below the radar. A Mexican named Hernandez and his sister Juanita. They pretty much had the entire Central Avenue area on lockdown. When those Federal Indictments came through Hernandez took the opportunity to expand his operation and expand he did.

Starting from Emmitt Street to Harrisburg one way and to Lake Almstead the other way. Even with the GBI having to drop the charges. That little vacation had been enough for Hernandez to flex his muscles. No one knew exactly what he was touching, but evidence suggested that he had a lot. It seemed like he was moving other Mexicans to Augusta, too. Either way, Hernandez and Juanita weren't small time. Even Young said they might just be some animals, too.

From what Dawg admitted after questioning Hernandez and found out he was seeing a Hispanic girl over on Central Avenue which was one of the areas that some Mexicans began to move into. So, Hernandez controlled the whole area. It was never an odd thing for him to show up. Dawg said he'd often seen him pull up and kick it with the guys who worked for him. Not all of them were Mexican some were black. Hernandez was a flashy guy, pushing different types of rides, from the ole school box Chevys to the 2012 i8 BMW Coupe. All his old school rides looked like they came straight out of LowRider magazine. When Dawg saw the Coupe, he knew that it cost well over two-hundred grand, that's what impressed him. He'd also been hearing from his girl that Hernandez was looking for a good Lieutenant. At the time he wasn't aware of the fact that she was recruiting him for Hernandez.

After the GBI arrest, Young had them all tighten up in case something came next. It wasn't that Young Castro wasn't breaking bread. Young showed love, but none of them could say that they were riding a 2012 nothing and it was December of 2011. Young had been pushing this package for six months and Dawg felt like they should've been balling harder, but Young had everybody on a diet. Considering the amount of coke they now had. He didn't want them drawing any more attention. Especially since Jasmine found out that the FBI had a serious hard-on for him, like a groupie.

So, Dawg was feeling like his shirt was buttoned up too tight. Thus, he started lusting after the finer things he saw Hernandez people with. Through his eyes he let the first devil come into his heart. Greed!

What Jeeta didn't understand with Young there was never a need to steal. The brother broke bread righteously. So, when the first report came that some of the product was short and that it looked as if the package had been open Jeeta disregarded it. Thinking that was impossible. Only five of them even knew about the coke. Out of the five, only three knew where it was buried. Young, himself, and Poe. Poe only knew because fresh out of the hospital Young didn't want him in the streets so soon. So, he'd become a runner, going to get the dope whenever Jeeta needed some. This was how Dawg found out where the dope was buried. Just like a rodent, always watching shit.

Having gotten nosey, he'd followed Poe twice. Poe hadn't been thinking to pay that kind of attention. After all, the coke was buried in the woods across the bridge in South Carolina.

After the second report, Jeeta decided to look into it himself. So, he set up a system with a camcorder that watched and recorded the area for 72 hours, using a digital chip. At first, when he looked at the recording, he hadn't seen anything. So, he fast-forwarded through a lot of the footage. Until he came to a section with movement. Jeeta slowed the images down and watched. Sure, enough a hooded figure went to the spot and dug up the coke.

He knew immediately that it wasn't Poe. Because Poe was still using a cane to walk and he walked with a limp. But this bitch ass nigga didn't. Jeeta watched trying to figure out who the nigga could be. He couldn't see his face. Jeeta watched as he went to the spot and pulled out one of the bricks of cocaine. He opened it then used another bag that he had. He shook some of the coke out of the package into the bag. He then resealed the package and did the same thing with three others. Only taking a little from each one.

It wasn't until he finished and was about to leave that Jeeta got a flash of his face. At first, he didn't believe it, he had replayed it several times to be sure. But yeah that was exactly who it was.

Jeeta looked across the room at the muthafucka as he screamed again from the whip's lash. Young had made Poe the one responsible for the beating. Since he was the one Dawg had followed. He should have been more careful.

"Stupid ass, nigga," Jeeta mumbled again. "You never bite the hand that feeds you. Especially when you were eating with animals at the table."

There was a difference between a zoo and a jungle. At a zoo, the animals were tamed and caged. These animals couldn't get to you. After enough time went by, they grew to accept their positions. Until something changed all they could do was look at you, while in captivity waiting.

But in the jungle, there were no cages and the animals weren't forced into submission. None of them were tamed and they didn't have to depend on anyone other than themselves for food. In the jungle, there were no rules. At the zoo, the animals were fed. While in the jungle these animals hunt one another to eat.

Right now, Jeeta was watching the animal Poe as he ate. While next to him sat the silent lion, He was the panther waiting to pounce. The screams came from the hyena every time the gorilla struck.

Yeah, he thought. *This is the jungle and the law is self-preservation. Only the strong will be able to survive.*

Survival was the overall goal in the jungle. Especially if you wanted to be successful. This was Thug Life, and these were Animal Thugs.

Chapter Two

2005 EAST NEW YORK

A Memory

"A'ight lil' nigga. This is what I need you to do." Young Cas looked up at Jameen as he spoke.

He really hated being over here in Pink Houses. Actually, he hated all East New York, and it wasn't because he was hating on the area. It was because this area was the slum. It was infested with drug addicts, crime, and poverty to the highest degree. It was once said that if you wanted to really teach a green nigga how to hustle. There were two places you could send him. East New York or Harlem, in both places it seemed like some of the people, didn't even realize just how bad they were, or how bad they really had it.

"Go on up there to apartment 5D," Jameen explained to him. "When you knock on the door and somebody answers. You say Prophet sent you."

Young Cas waited but it didn't seem like he was about to say anything else. He hunched his shoulders then turned and walked toward the building he'd been shown. There weren't too many things he was scared of. When he reached the building, he went inside. Then took the staircases up. On the second landing, he came across a couple of heroin addicts who looked to be in a bad way. One of them was nodding with a nearly burnt-out cigarette hanging from the corner of his mouth.

The other one was shaking like a stripper. That was the main reason he hated East New York. Ever since his moms had started getting high, he developed a bad feeling toward junkies and it got worse when she overdosed.

Young Cas found his way up to apartment 5D. He knocked, then waited.

"Yeah!" someone hollered from the other side of the door.

"Aye, Prophet sent me," he called out.

There was a moment's silence, then he heard the door chains being removed and the deadbolts being unlocked. When the door opened, he found himself facing a big, dark-skinned gorilla who had a lot of bumps in his face. Young Cas watched as the nigga stuck his head out the door and looked both ways. Up and down each hallway, then he looked back at Young Cas. It was also at this point Young Cas saw the large .357 in the niggas left hand. Young Cas had seen plenty of guns, so he wasn't scared. Nor did the gorilla scare him.

"The fuck Jameen send a green nigga up here?" The nigga cursed. Then looked Young Cas up and down. "Yo', you God?" he asked.

This was the most common question asked in all of New York. When you were seen with or known to be with the Gods. Other than them there were the Muslims. It was the Nation of Gods and Earths who were the most righteous of individuals in New York streets and a few of the Zulu nation people.

Not all the Gods were perfect. There were a lot of 5 *pretenders* too. Niggaz who straddled the fence trying to be God, hustlers, gang bangers, and in some cases junkies. Those were the ways of man that they didn't want to let go. That wasn't their teachings.

"Nah, I'm just me," Young Cas stated.

"Yeah, a'ight." He smacked his lips. "Come on in, *Just Me.*"

The ugly nigga stepped back to let him enter. The apartment wasn't all that big. Young Cas wasn't even surprised. He saw all types of guns and drugs lying around the room in various places.

"Yo, hold up, let me get that for you," Ugly said.

Young Cas waited while he closed the door and went to one of the back rooms. While he waited, he looked around the room, then his eyes stopped when they landed on the coffee table. Seeing the glass crack pipe, the spoon, and the needle along with the other junkie tools, his mind had a sudden flashback.

$$$$

"Oh, shit—ooohhh shit-shit-shit," the woman chanted as she rocked back and forth sitting on the edge of the ragged sofa.

The t-shirt she wore smelled like piss and hadn't been washed in weeks. The shorts she had on were even worse. Her hair, which had once consisted of long lustrous curls. Now boasted of broken ends and tangles of naps. Her eyes were sunken in and ringed with dark flesh around them. She'd lost so much weight and her skin was ashen.

"Good shit. That's good shit—good—shit," she sang.

The rubber band was still tied around her arm, but the needle now laid on the coffee table. In its midst were also a crack pipe, a few lighters, and other tools. The woman didn't even see the twelve-year-old little boy. He stood at the doorway behind her. Having just come out of his room. He'd gotten hungry, and even though he knew there wasn't any real food in the house. There was still the large chunk of government cheese she hadn't been able to sell. Nobody ever brought the cheese and he was always thankful for that. He knew that it was sitting inside of the refrigerator, which had been his destination until he came across the scene before him.

He looked at the woman and took in the tracks that ran up and down her arms. He'd seen enough junkies out in the parks and stairways to know the signs.

"Boy that's good shit!" she continued to chant.

He stood there, hungry and staring, but wasn't scared. He was never scared of life.

$$$$

"Ayo, you hear me, lil nigga?" Ugly asked.

Young Cas shook the memory off. "Nah, what—you say?" he asked and watched as Ugly stood there looking at him in a strange way as if he was the one lost in thought.

"Fuckin' mental health ass niggas Jameen keeps around him," he mumbled. "But yo, tell that nigga—" He smacked his lips. Young Cas now noticed that they were ashy white and Ugly looked like he might be tasting his own shit. "Tell him, he still owes me for the last time. Tell that nigga don't be playing wit' my dough," he explained, then held out the bag.

Young Cas took the bag, he wasn't even about to look into it. He already had an idea what it was. "Yeah, a'ight, I'll tell him," he said, then turn to the door.

****

"We were taught by the Honorable Elijah Muhammad that the black man is the Original man. The Maker, the Owner, cream of the planet Earth. Father of Civilization and God of the Universe."

Jameen was in the process of explaining while they sat inside the kitchen. Young listened to every word the older man spoke. He knew that the History Jameen spoke came to the shores of North America for the upliftment of black people as

24

a Nation. His ears heard that and took it in. His eyes observed the moral contradiction in front of him. Jameen sat across the table from him. In one hand he held a box cutter, while on the table in front of him was the 14.5 grams of cocaine.

Actually, it was crack now since he'd cooked it up. Jameen had just taught him how to cook it. He was now showing him how it was supposed to be cut, while at the same time teaching him what he said was *truth and righteousness*.

Young never could understand why jive percenters made a righteous culture look bad. People like Jameen most definitely weren't a five percenter. A real five percenter strives for righteousness and wouldn't intentionally compromise his integrity for the devil's luxuries. They weren't perfect and some of them might fall along the way or stumble here and there. They didn't make excuses for those stumbles and try to justify them. While a jive percenter knew the lessons and would try to use them to do just that, make excuses for their ways and actions.

If you watched their ways and actions, you would eventually be able to see the devilment and see through the bullshit. They sold drugs and disrespected women belligerently. Then tried to explain why they were still righteous. Young had seen this many times. None of these guys were trying to do better. He'd even seen some who smoked crack and would try to make it sound like they were mastering the devilment. They even made it sound like the white man-made them inhale. Young knew bullshit when he smelled it. He'd never been to the country a day in his life.

"You see son, the true nature of the black family is that of a holy existence," Jameen stated.

And you out here selling crack, telling people you God, Young thought, but never spoke his thoughts.

Instead, he listened and learned because he'd come to realize that even a black devil could tell you the truth. At the same time, he thought about his own views of the crack hustle. To him, it was just a means by which he could make money. Young could care less about who chooses to smoke it. Black, white, Hispanic, Chinese, he didn't care. The only thing he wouldn't do was sell it to a pregnant woman or a kid. To him, that was just too much evil.

Jameen continued to explain how black people in Egypt were once Kings, Queens, and Gods or Goddess. Young reflected over all those times he'd had to go to bed hungry. Having to wake up in the middle of the night, stomach twisted. Having to drink water just to make it to the next day. Or the times he'd hung around the back of Bodegas waiting for them to throw away the food they hadn't sold that day.

If he begged just the right way, they wouldn't throw it in the garbage. They'd sit it somewhere and walk back inside. Sort of how you'd feed dogs or cats. It was those nights when he would take some of the food back home and force his mom to eat it. Those were the nights his heart hurt the most and his pride took the back seat, while hunger rode up front.

She would eat the food, while his mind would eat the knowledge of their true reality. Those nights took away his fears. He used to fear the dark. When night fell and he was hungry. Young didn't think too many people in New York that was his age had it as rough.

He'd often spent the better parts of the nights in tears. Reflecting over that day's struggle. He'd learned to do three things. One, how to swallow his pride. Two, how to swallow his pain. Three, to love the taste of his fears, as he swallowed those, too. Thus, the making of an Animal.

$$$$

The housing authorities eventually found out that he'd been living in the apartment by himself. After all, he had no way to pay the rent. So, the day they came for him, he'd ran. That's how he met *Jameen the Prophet*. By running into another building as the cops chased him. Jameen's baby's mother held the door open so that he could run inside and hide. He got away that day, but she was pregnant and had a house full of kids. Young couldn't see himself taking food out of their mouths.

Jameen eventually set it up so that he could sleep inside one of his crack houses. The arrangement worked both ways actually. He needed to be sure his workers weren't bullshitting and fucking up the work. So, he eventually started having Young hold the work for them. Which meant less excuses for the cops got behind me, so I had to toss the work. Or somebody stole the work out of the stash spot.

Young needed a place to sleep and a way to eat. So, he got to eat white castles twice a day and had an alright bed to sleep in. He went to bed with a full stomach most nights. Sometimes he'd lay there and listen to the workers. Tonight, they were arguing over an outfit one of the smokers had boosted. While all of this was going on Young thought about his life. How fucked up it really was. These were the nights he told himself. That once he was older, he would find a better way. He often had dreams about having the finer things in life.

Then he thought, while he liked the knowledge. He couldn't be God's body. His head was just too fucked up to be righteous and he couldn't gangbang. Most of those niggaz loyalties were suspect, but he did respect the heart of some of them. Instead, he would borrow from both.

He promised himself if he was ever given the chance to get his weight up. He would never allow himself to sink so low again. To him, this was the lowest point that his life would ever reach. It made him feel like more than one animal. A gorilla, a wolf, and a panther. He couldn't be a lion, because a lion was a king. Right now, he didn't feel like a king. He most definitely felt like a hungry animal. Maybe he would grow up to be a lion one day. Just not today, today he was a hybrid predator.

Chapter Three

Augusta, GA—2011

"Nah, fuck that, Pah," Young Castro spoked into the new cellphone he'd purchased yesterday.

The whole time he was whipping through traffic in the new 2011 Denali that was midnight blue with 24-inch pinnacle blade rims. In the background, the smooth sounds of *Al Green's* song *For The Good Times* could be heard clearly.

At the moment he was caught up in what the other person was saying, "I'm trying to fuck wit' ya Pah. But you giving me an ulcer son."

"Listen, Castro," Juggernaut said on the other end of the phone. "I can do one, but I'm not in any shape to be buying two cakes, right now. Bruh, you know a nigga got bills. If I could, I would. No hesitation, bruh. Serious," he stressed.

Young Castro made a left at the light. He was on his way to meet Poe. But then Juggernaut called trying to renegotiate their deal.

"Look, Pah, my people already got both cakes in the oven. So, tell me, how we gon' take it out and remix it? Does that make sense to you son?" he asked on the other end of the phone Juggernaut was silent. Young Castro could hear him breathing.

They were both trying to find a logical solution to the problem. Since Juggernaut had gotten out of jail he'd had to move his shop. He was over in Fox Den now, which used to be called Stone Gate. Because he had a female out there the other niggaz weren't giving him too much of a problem.

"A'ight, Pah, how 'bout we freak it like this," Young Castro began. "We hit you wit' both cakes, give you the chance to do your thing, right? And ya owe me some more dough. But here's the hook, when you come back you bring my dough. And you buy three more Betty Crockers. You smell me on that son?"

He turned into Sunsetvilla and came around until he found what he was looking for. "Damn, bruh, you gon' fuck with me like that?" Juggernaut asked, surprised.

"Hold up—hold up," Young Castro said into the phone. "Look son, this is what I need you to understand. I don't mind putting niggaz on in the hustle. In truth, I need more niggaz on a certified level," he explained.

Outside he could see people going in and out of the apartment. Poe had a nice set up over here. Almost as good as the one Cream had in Governors Place, but Cream had too much going on out that way.

"But listen to me good, Pah," Young Castro continued. "You ain't gon' get but one shot. That's all you gon' get, son. You fuck that up. You play wit' my dough and it's a wrap. Niggaz might twist yo' biscuit."

"Look, Thug," Juggernaut said. "You fuck wit' me like that and we won't have no problems. And that's Thug life fo' real."

Young Castro didn't say anything. He had learned in life especially in the streets. Niggaz would say a whole lot of shit when things were going their way, but as soon as they fucked up, it would be some other shit altogether. Either way, he still needed people who could move big weight. Considering the amount of coke, he was getting, he couldn't sit on it for too long.

$$$$

"Girl, don't make me put my foot in yo ass," Poe called back to his girl Nana.

At the moment she was standing in the doorway of her apartment talking shit. From what he could tell, she was throwing a fit because he'd eaten the last of her kids' Fruit Loops. When he got up, she'd still had her lazy ass in the bed and he wasn't about to try cooking shit. The way he saw it, niggaz really didn't have no business in the kitchen anyway. He completed the sale he'd been in the process of making. Then was about to tell her he'd buy some more cereal. When he looked up and saw the Denali enter the parking lot.

"Ayo, Tech," he called out to one of his workers.

Tech-9 turned from making a sell of his own. "Yeah. What's up, Thug?" he asked.

Him being originally from Augusta, he was part of the local Augusta movement that the young thugs had started called LOE, *Loyalty Over Everything.*

"I'll be back in a minute," Poe said. "Wifey needs some things from the store. So, hold the spot down."

"I got it, Thug, do you," Tech 9 said. Then he turned and started issuing orders to the other three niggaz who worked for Poe.

Poe on the other hand held a finger up to Young Castro. Then he bounced back to the apartment where Nana was still talking shit. "Look, ma, I'm about to go get a few boxes of cereal for the kids. You need anything else?" he asked, then watched as she sucked her teeth and rolled her head on her shoulders, but she didn't say anything.

Poe kissed her on the lips and then turned. Nana was one of those for real hood chicks. She stood about 5'6 and was extra thick. The girl had hips like a racehorse and she had a creamy brown skin tone. She only had two kids which Poe treated like his own.

"Yo, what you got going on, Pah?" Young Castro asked, seeing as Poe had just opened the door and jumped in.

"Not much, son. Ayo, run me to the grocery store right quick, Wifey PMSing," Poe stated.

It wasn't like he had to say a whole lot after that. Young knew how that shit was. There were times when Raine got on the bullshit, too, but lately, she'd been alright. Seeing as he'd moved her into that big ass house right down from Francis and Jazmine. Plus, that three-thousand-dollar rock he placed on her hand.

"A'ight." Young backed the Denali up and then turned back into the street. "So how that business looking, Pah?" He asked.

"Business is good, I mean it is now anyway," Poe corrected himself.

After that issue with Dawg, he'd had some straightening up to do. He got everything into its fit formation and once they buried the body it was back to business.

"A'ight, so we gon' be good on that next move then," Young stated as he whipped the SUV through traffic. "Because I already got Jeeta on point, and Cream is ready. So, the question, right now, Pah, is are you ready?"

Poe took a moment to think over the statement. After the situation with Dawg, he didn't think he would ever be right again. Not because of what Young made him do to Dawg, but because of their history. They'd literally grown up together.

"Yeah, yeah, son," Poe said. "I'ma be ready." Young nodded.

What he was about to do would put all his team on front street. Since listening to the shit that Dawg had said. He'd decided to step it up a notch. Meaning that he was giving them even more weight. This next shipment would place each one of them at kingpin status with the Feds. However, with so much product coming in, Young needed a larger team. He was even thinking about pulling both Ace and Juggernaut into the immediate cipher. He just had to talk to Jeeta before he did that.

$$$$

"That nigga, Money Loc," Jeeta said as the black-on-black Excursion pulled into the parking lot and the driver hopped out.

At the moment they were all parked in Lake Almsted apartments. Jeeta had been sitting on the front stoop of the apartment he lived in with Crystal and their daughter. He was surprised actually that Money Loc had pulled up and parked behind his new sky-blue Range Rover Sport. Because it wasn't like they were that cool for the nigga to be pulling up at his spot. Money Loc was a big nigga. He stood every bit of 6'3 and weighed something like 340lbs. He was built like a football player. Because he too was a Crip, he rocked the color blue, only he rocked a darker blue.

"What's cracking, cuz?" Money Loc asked.

Causing Jeeta to look at him slightly sideways. Out west, their two sets didn't rock with one another. Since Jeeta had been in Augusta he'd made it known that he didn't fake kick it. There were several rumors in the streets that Money Loc talked bad about him behind his back. Nevertheless, being cordial about it.

"It ain't much, cuz. What you up to?" Jeeta asked.

He waited while Money Loc stood there and glanced around. There were several niggaz out there trapping good at the moment.

"Listen, cuz," Money Loc began. "Word on the streets is you about to have problems with this Mexican nigga," he said.

"You mean, Hernandez?" Jeeta said.

"Yeah, any truth to that, cuz?" Money Loc asked.

Jeeta tipped his head as if he was looking up at the grey clouds in the sky above. He was trying to figure out why Money Loc had pulled up in the first place. If he had an issue with the Mexicans, it wasn't like Money Loc and his set were going to step up and ride with him. Not that he expected them to.

"I don't have problems, cuz," Jeeta said.

He watched as Money Loc looked at him almost as if he expected something else. "Well here's the thing, cuz." Money Loc stated. "Me and my homies got business with these cats. We've been getting some pretty good deals on the coke from them. And we don't need them thinking they beefing with Rollin 20s."

Ah, Jeeta thought as he listened. *These niggaz trying to play the middleman. Trying to save face with the people they were in business with.* "Nah, cuz, it ain't no beef. Or at least I haven't heard that it was—" Jeeta said, then paused. "But on the real, though. I'm Hoover, and we don't answer to you and your homies."

Jeeta and Crystal were both from Hoover Street which was known mostly as Hoover Gangster Crip. They weren't too friendly with any of the neighborhoods such as 60s and 20s. Who were real big in Augusta. He watched as Money Loc twisted his face up almost as if he wanted to say something.

"Chill, homie, me and mine ain't at your throat. We just trying to protect our investment. That's all," he explained.

"Well, since you've invested in those spics. Shouldn't you be presenting your argument to them?" Jeeta asked.

"I just wanted to make sure there weren't any misunderstandings," Money Loc stated. Then watched as Jeeta laughed.

"Trust me, cuz—" Jeeta began. "There would never be any misunderstandings. Niggaz in the streets knows the difference between me and your people. Other than my lady, there ain't but four original Hoover Gangsters in Augusta.

He knew that was a well-known fact. There was a Hoover set put down in Augusta, but the Crips who were in it were locals. The four original Hoover Gangster Crips he mentioned were his personal people. Trap Loc, Amp Loc, and his lady Sheba and the older head, OG Issac. None of whom even fucked with the neighborhood sets.

"A'ight, cuz, I'ma pull-up," Money Loc said.

Jeeta watched as he turned and threw his hood up. Then walked back to his ride. Jeeta began thinking, *This nigga's gonna be a problem.*

$$$$

Money Loc slid back in and behind the wheel. He started the Excursion and pulled off. "Ole tough-ass nigga," he mumbled.

The real reason he'd pulled up was because one of his lil' homies that was Mexican came to him. He'd said that Hernandez wanted to be sure that there wouldn't be any set tripping with the whole C-Nation if he stepped to this nigga Jeeta. Hernandez said Jeeta was in his way. He and this Young Castro. They were doing too much.

"I don't like them New York niggaz, anyway," he mumbled.

His real issue was with these Hoover niggaz. They thought just because they were from California and were gangbanging first that niggaz on the East Coast weren't banging right. Ever since these niggaz been in Augusta they'd been acting funny. Like their shit don't stink. Or other niggaz gunz don't clap.

"Well, Hernandez is about to see what this niggaz G is like," he said to himself. Then looked up into his own eyes in the rearview. "Straight Up."

Chapter Four

A Memory

Harlem N.Y.

"Peace to the God," the greeting caused Jameen's head to turn, he looked around and saw the tall dark-skinned brother with eight-inch dreadlocks rocking the Coogi sweater and blue jeans.

"Peace Allah!" Jameen greeted Elevation as he came to a stop next to them.

At that moment Jameen had been talking with one of his workers. They'd just left a cipher that the Gods and Earths had held in the park earlier. Now they were standing on 7th Avenue talking. He hadn't seen Elevation at the cipher and kind of intended not to see his self-righteous ass.

"I ain't seen you in a while, G'. How you living?" Elevation asked.

His eyes took in the whole situation as he came to a standstill. His eyes took in the heroin junkie that Jameen was talking to. This junkie was actually well known. He was said to have good hustling skills. As long as you didn't give him any boy to move.

"Life is good out in Medina," Jameen said. "Just came out here to introduce my seed to a few of the Gods." He nodded to where Young Cas stood silently.

Young Cas was far from stupid, he noticed the way this new God pulled up. How he looked at all three of them. It seemed like his mind was calculating the whole situation.

"Yo' seed, huh?" Elevation focused his sight on Young Cas as he spoke. "Peace, God. Who you be?"

"I'm just me," Young Cas said.

He was already familiar with the way the Gods would pull up on one another and question them right there on the spot.

"He ain't got no name yet," Jameen put in.

"A'ight, so what he know?" Elevation asked.

"A lil bit of the Math and Bets. But I'm still working on him," Jameen stated.

Elevation looked from him back to Young Cas. He wanted to say something but didn't. Like everyone else, he knew that Jameen wasn't the right one to be teaching. Because Jameen was in essence a Black Devil that wore God's clothes. Many people didn't understand the Five Percenters like that. They assume that when they saw a Jive Pretender who professed to be God. That these were really representatives of the culture. Whereas, in truth, they weren't. They were far from that image.

"Well, I'm about to head up to the school. You should swing by with your seed," Elevation said.

"Yeah, yeah, I might just do that," Jameen said.

Elevation knew he wouldn't, brothers like Jameen didn't like being around a lot of Gods and Earths. Because it was harder to manipulate a lot of people. They would instead keep smaller circles and manipulate those they infect. Elevation turned and started walking off in the direction of Allah's School.

$$$$

Young Cas watched the other God leave. As he left his attention was drawn back to the situation with Jameen and the Junkie.

"Like I was saying, nigga. Where the fuck my shit at? And I don't wanna hear no dumb shit either," Jameen stressed.

Young Cas watched as the Junkie looked all spooked out. His eyes shifted from Jameen to him.

"Duke, listen to me," the Junkie started to repeat what he'd said before Elevation pulled up. "It was that bald-headed nigga that looked like that rappin' nigga DMX," the Junkie said. "But this nigga wasn't a dark nigga. He was about a shade lighter than you. Yo, Duke ran up on me with the heater out."

Young Cas watched as the nigga became animated and even made hand gestures like he held a gun. "The nigga was like. Yo, yo, nigga, where dat shit at? Where it at nigga?" the Junkie repeated. "And I'm like, yooo, Duke, you know this shit right here. This shit belongs to, Prophet," he stated looking at Jameen all cross-eyed. "Then the nigga like, Son, who da fuck is a Prophet? Don't nobody give a damn 'bout dat Brooklyn nigga. Yo, we in Harlem, right now. Nigga cough dat shit up before I split yo' cabbage," the Junkie detailed the robbery to them. "And Duke listened, "he continued. "I'm not about to take no slug for no nigga."

Young Cas watched as Jameen stood there and then glanced around. He was still an Animal in training. So, he had to pay close attention to the way Jameen handled these types of situations.

"Fuck that, nigga. What if I was gon' put a slug in yo' ass? Fuck that DMX look-alike nigga. I'm the muthafuckin' threat," Jameen stated, but even as he said it, Young Cas could tell that he wasn't about to kill the Junkie. It wasn't worth the trouble.

$$$$

"Ayo Son, listen carefully, "Jameen said.

It was now nightfall and they were standing up the street from an apartment building on 8th Avenue. This was where the junkie said the jack boy lived.

"We gon' rush up in this spot. But we ain't gon' play no games, "Jameen stated. "You got yo' piece?" he asked. Young Cas lifted the 4 XL starter jersey that he wore. Showing the handle of the .38 special.

"Yo', you just watch my back. Let me do all the gangsta shit when we get up in there," he said.

The whole time Young Cas stood there trembling. He wasn't scared, because he wasn't scared of shit. Young Cas was cold. It was the middle of November and in New York, the wind blew pretty hard. The cold air usually came in off the bay. Making the average night even colder.

"A'ight lil', nigga. Let's go get my money back." Jameen turned and walked toward the side of the building where the fire escape was.

There wasn't any need to try the door. These old buildings had a rebar inside which would reinforce the door. Making it impossible to kick the door in. Young Cas watched as Jameen pulled out the cold blue steel 9mm, while he reached under his sweater and removed the .38 Jameen had given him. They were now standing in the back of the building looking up at the fire escape.

$$$$

"Bitch," the Jackboy that sat on the sofa in front of the coffee table said. He was hunched forward, bent over the table. At the moment he was weighing the cocaine that he'd just struck for. His next step would be to cook it, then cut it. "I thought I told you to go down to the corner store and cop me a box of Arm-N-Hammer?" he stated. Then looked up as his girlfriend sucked her teeth.

She wore a nice full-length dress that he'd gotten off one of the boosters a week ago. She was fine to him. A little thick around the waist, but the girl had a nice ass.

The Jack boy was about to repeat himself when she rolled both her neck and her eyes. Then she grabbed her purse and started out the door. He shook his head because he knew why she was mad. He still owed her five-hundred dollars on last month's bills and she was eyeing the role of big faces that also sat on the table. But he wasn't about to come up off no loot just yet. He still had to—

"What the fuck was that?" The Jack boy stopped mid-thought.

His girl had already left and he knew there wasn't anyone else in the building. He stopped what he was doing and cocked his head to the side, listening for other noises. The .357 lay on the table right in front of him, but he didn't reach for it. After two full minutes of silence, he assumed that what he thought he heard was only in his mind, not the apartment. Just as he reached for the scale again he heard another noise. Almost the same as the last noise.

"What the fuck?" he cursed out loud.

His words fell short as he turned his head toward the bedrooms and froze. Standing right there in the hallway was another nigga holding a pistol in his left hand.

The gun, at the moment, was pointed downward, along his side. The Jack boy had a moment's hesitation. Then he turned and reached for the .357. His body moved all at once. His hand barely touched the gun when a shot rang out and the pain ran through his shoulder.

"Aaahhhh," Jack boy cried out.

"Don't move, muthafucka!" Jameen shouted as he stepped further into the room. "Don't you muthafuckin' move, nigga," he continued.

Jack boy fell sideways on the sofa clutching his arm. The pain was killing him now. He looked up into the shooter's face. He also noticed there was a young kid with him. The kid stood there, just watching.

"Yo', Young, check the apartment. Make sure there isn't anybody else here. Then bar that door," he said.

Jameen held the 9mm aimed at the Jackboy while Young Cas went about checking the apartment. He was giving the nigga who'd stolen his shit the evil eye. His eyes took in the money that sat on the table.

My money, he thought.

"It's clean," Young Cas stated as he came back into the front room.

Jameen looked the nigga in the eyes. "Yo', you ain't know who you was stealing from?" he asked with a serious expression on his face. He watched as the nigga still clutched his shoulder. Jameen didn't feel no kind of way about it. "Nigga, I'm the muthafuckin', Prophet. Don't nobody fuck wit' my shit."

"Fuck you, nigga," Jackboy stated. "Niggaz saying you ain't even God body in the streets. You a fucking black devil, nigga." Jack boy looked into Jameen's twisted gaze.

Then his eyes shifted to Young Cas. He'd heard it in the streets that this nigga Prophet Jameen was claiming to be a Five Percenter, but he was really poison to the culture. Word was, the Gods hadn't taken him out because they didn't want to cause a conflict, but he took it as an excuse to rob the niggaz workers.

"Oh, yeah. "Jameen smiled. "That's what niggaz in the streets is saying? He watched Jack boy spit on the floor right at his feet. A true sign of disrespect. "Well, guess what nigga?" Jameen raised and aimed the gun. "If I'm the devil, nigga, then I'ma send you to hell so you can look after my affairs until I get back." He laughed. Then squeezed the trigger.

$$$$

They caught the train and were on their way back to East New York. Young Cas had been quiet ever since the shooting inside of the apartment. Jameen assumed that it could only be one of two things. Either he was shook about seeing him kill the nigga, or he was thinking about the shit the nigga had said to him. About him being a black devil. Prophet really didn't think Young Cas was shook up about seeing the bodywork. So, it had to be the other issue.

"Listen young, nigga." He leaned sideways to say. They were sitting next to one another on the train. "You might be wondering why that nigga called me a devil? But I think the nigga had his issues wrong," he stated, formulating his trick-knowledge as he spoke. Young Cas gave his undivided attention. Because he really did want to hear how he explained this one. "You see, the word devil means one who's grafted from the original. Made weak and wicked by the process. And doesn't have original thoughts. Why you think it doesn't call Yacub a devil in the lessons. It calls him the Father of the devil. It says Yacub was an Original Blackman born twenty miles outside the Holy City Mecca," He half quoted the lesson which Young Cas had seen, but he wasn't necessarily on those degrees yet.

Young Cas thought about what Jameen said as he glanced around. He saw a guy that looked like he was close to being homeless. This guy sat across from them, it looked like he'd been listening to Jameen speak. Young Cas looked the man in the eyes. Something about him seemed to stand out. Young knew that it wasn't his dress code. He laughed inside. The brown-skinned brother looked like he found his clothes at a Salvation Army or something.

Upon closer inspection, it didn't look like the guy was under fed. Then there was that real intense look in his eyes. Young Cas could still hear Jameen building as he tried to make what the nigga in the apartment said sound like he was the crazy one. As he spoke Young Cas held this brown-skinned brother's eyes. He noticed that the man's hands were clean. He knew this because his fingernails weren't dirty. All the bums he knew had dirty nails. He also saw that, while the brother had nappy hair. It looked clean. Almost as if he were about to start growing dreads.

"So, it's the ten-percent that are the rich bloodsuckers of the poor. That being your preachers and politicians. Me—" Jameen paused to look down at him. "I'm just living brother. I'm only out here providing a service for those who gon' get it anyway. So, shit we all gotta eat. I don't think that makes me a devil. I'm not forcing anyone to smoke crack I'm just making sure I benefit if they do decide to. Nothing more, nothing less God," Jameen stated.

Young Cas nodded his head, letting him know that he understood what he was saying, but with his eyes. Young Cas watched as the brother across from them shook his head. He was letting it be known that Jameen was twisting his words.

Chapter Five

"The fuck is up, nigga? Thug life bitch." Ace sat and watched as the group of niggaz walked away from the basketball court.

He didn't really get into playing sports a lot. Before he'd gone to juvy he'd played football at the Rec Center, but doing time somehow changed his perspective. Prison had been filled with fuck niggaz, homosexuals, fags, and more. Even though he always thought because he wasn't gay. The experiences of other people didn't affect him. He couldn't have been more wrong. The truth was an ugly pill to swallow.

He'd been sent to Milledgeville YDC and when he left the Augusta YDC and made it to the new one. He didn't really think much of it. When he first made it to general population, they put him in the room with a fuck nigga which wasn't really a problem. As long as the nigga kept the bullshit on his side of the room.

He had learned that most of the niggaz who acted too tough and gay-bashed on the punks were some of the same niggaz who would be falling off in duck off spots with the sissy to get straight. He was even surprised to see some of the gang members trembling around, but he didn't say anything. Those gang niggaz were more sensitive than the bitches that raised them. The slightest perceived insult and they'd mount up like a bunch of hoes on Love & Hip Hop.

The room situation didn't last long though. Shit got serious when he saw the fuck nigga put M&Ms candy on his lips for lipstick and wear a laundry bag that had been made into a fishnet type dress. Ace just couldn't take it, so he beat his roommate up and was sent to the box.

He watched as the basketball niggaz disappeared from his line of vision. He'd been sitting on the bleachers at Hunter Center which was at the bottom of Sunset. He held his left arm

45

up and checked the time on his Swarovski watch. Ace was waiting for Young Castro to pull up. Because he really needed this plug. He'd never had a real plug before. In fact, his big step in the dope game came via YDC, too.

When he beat his roommate up, they sent him to the Box which was a lockdown unit. It was while he'd been in the box that he met this nigga Dollas. Another young nigga from Atlanta. Ace really didn't like the nigga, especially with him being well over six-feet-tall and 220lbs and he had the nerve to keep calling him, "Shawty."

On top of all that, the nigga talked too much. For everything Ace said, he always seemed to have a better story to tell. It was almost as if he would wait for Ace to say something. Then he'd have a better way to tell a similar story. Probably got the shit out of one of those hood books. Because he always had a complete story to tell. Urban book ass nigga.

The nigga was always bragging about how much dope he sold. His Escalade or the big house he'd brought for his moms when he was just fifteen-years-old. The nigga was just fuckin' incredible! He did all this shit in such a short life span. The shit used to put him to sleep at night. Nursery rhymes and shit.

For some strange reason, two days before he was supposed to get out of the hole. This nigga Dollas started talking about how he'd buried some dope in his mother's back yard. Ace thought the nigga was flexin, so he'd overlooked it. The very next day, though. The nigga started yapping again. This time he asked when Ace was going home.

Turned out he would be getting out six months before. So, he gave Ace his mother's address and told him to come up to the A. At that point, Ace knew the nigga was capped up. But he accepted the address anyway. Thinking he'd throw it away later, but when they let him out of the hole. They put him in a dorm that had a lot of his homeboys from Augusta in it. They were on that LOE Life shit hard. Either way, niggaz rolled up blunts and twisted Bombays. So, he eventually forgot about the address. In fact, he forgot about the nigga Dollas altogether. Until two weeks later, the whole YDC was placed on lockdown for three whole days. When they finally got off, Inmate.com had the official changing news.

Word in the streets was, over in the thunder dorm some nigga got shanked up by some Bloods and died. Ace kept hearing a name, but it was some niggaz government name. The story was, the young nigga pulled a sneak robbery somewhere in Atlanta when he was twelve or thirteen. They said he saw where some niggaz hid their work, and when the GBI game through on a raid and locked niggaz up. This young nigga went back and lifted their work.

A few years went by and the young nigga flipped the work several times over. He got his weight up and started doing big things. Nobody knew how this young nigga came up. As it so happened, the people that the work belonged to were from somewhere upstate. They put the word out that they were missing some product, but this lil nigga wasn't hustling out of the same neighborhood. He'd moved down to College Park. Nobody but his family knew him down there.

It was when Inmate.com said that one of the G-Shine homies were in the hole next door to the nigga and since the walls were thin. He overheard the nigga talking to his roommate. Then he recognized a few of the street names that were mentioned. He began putting the pieces together. The time frame was right. The work that went missing had belonged to his uncle. That was when Ace began to realize they were talking about Dollas.

Ace looked up when the Denali pulled into the parking lot and parked. He saw Young Castro step out and turn to walk toward him. Jeeta exited on the passenger side only a moment later. He pushed his youthful memories aside. After all, that had been three years ago. Ace had gotten out and gone to Atlanta, where he dug up the two kilos that Dollas buried. Those same two bricks had solidified his standing in the game, but he had a hard time moving up to anything larger. Mostly because he'd had no plug. So, he'd had to buy packages. That was then, now he was fucking with these niggaz.

$$$$

"Here's the thing, Pah," Young Castro said. He and Jeeta were now sitting on the bleachers along with Ace. "I'ma need you to buy nothing short of five cakes at a time. Now if you need a start-up, cool. We can put that into motion. But the goal is to have you niggaz pushing ten bricks every re-up," he explained.

"Damn that's a lot of work, thug," Ace stated. He wasn't really questioning the program. He knew now that Young Castro and Jeeta were major and he didn't ask questions. He just appreciated the plug.

"Can you handle it, Pah? "Young Castro asked.

"Yeah," Ace stated. "I mean, I'ma have to shut down some of these low budget niggaz in the set. But once I bring out the new shit, it shouldn't be a problem."

Young Castro nodded. Then looked at Jeeta. "We good, son?" he asked.

"We good," Jeeta stated, but he looked to Ace. "You gon' need any help removing these niggaz?" he asked.

They waited as Ace gave it some thought. "I shouldn't," he stated. "But if I do, I'll give you a call." Jeeta nodded.

$$$$

"It's about time you brought yo' ass home," Raine stated as Young walked through the front door.

"Don't start, ma, "he said.

The house they now lived in was quite spacious. It held five bedrooms upstairs. Three ½ baths, a den, a kitchen, both living and dining rooms, and a laundry room. There was a large backyard that was fenced in and was more than enough room for the kids to play in which they would need, especially, with her being pregnant with his second seed. Young gave her a kiss, then turned to head upstairs. Just as he did, Raine's phone rang.

"Yeah, what's up girl?" She'd already seen that it was Jazmine.

"Not much. About to drop this load in a few weeks." Jazmine laughed. She was pregnant too. Only a few months farther along than Raine.

"So, what's going on with you guys?" Jazmine asked.

Even though they now lived in the same neighborhood and only a few houses away. They didn't get to see much of one another these days.

Jazmine now spent a lot of time with her mother, getting ready for the baby. While Raine was busy with their son Casey and her own pregnancy. They talked about those issues for a minute.

"Francis wanted me to see if Young could come by the club this weekend?" Jazmine said.

"I'll pass the message to him. But girl, that nigga has been busy lately," Raine hinted.

She couldn't mention Young Castro's business over the phone. Because they all knew that the DEA had a hard-on for him these days.

"Tell him he'd better be safe, "Jazmine stated. Not that she really had to stress as much. Nowadays both Young Castro and Raine were like their extended family.

"Girl, that nigga hardheaded as fuck," Raine told her. "He don't really listen to shit I say. In fact, I think Francis might be the only nigga he will listen to."

There was a brief pause as Jazmine thought about it. "Okay, I'ma have Francis talk to him," she said, but the facts couldn't be discussed over the phone. So, they left it unsaid as to what Francis would talk to him about.

Chapter Six

A Memory

Brooklyn, NY

Forte Green Housing

Young Castro sat on the couch in a daze. Although he was high, his mind still seemed to process all the things that were going on around him. They were at a party that Jameen's sister threw. Young Castro wasn't really big on smoking weed, but since his 17th birthday was only a week away and Jameen had officially given him his own trap house just four days ago. He figured, why the fuck not? So, he was high off the purple stuff. Sitting there watching as the people around him carried on.

Jameen's older sister's name was Papi which was a funny ass nickname for a girl who had three kids. Her two oldest were over eighteen while the baby was thirteen. Papi was a dyke bitch, who's been dyking for the past seven years. Word on the streets was she'd had a bad experience with a nigga. The nigga doped her up and let his whole crew put the dick on her. Now Papi was the one putting the dick on bitches.

Even as he watched her move through the crowd, slapping women on their asses and rubbing a few coochies. Young Cas still couldn't see it. Papi was a bad bitch. She had some age on her, but you wouldn't know it just by looking. She wasn't one of those hardcore dyke bitches that tried to look like a nigga. Nah, she looked like a woman and even dressed like one.

But it was her reputation that held the streets in check. Papi was known for having a 10 ½ inch gold strap on. They said her fuck game was more serious than most niggaz. However, every time Young Cas's eyes found her in the crowded apartment, he just wasn't seeing her as a dyke. Especially wearing the dress she had on tonight. Papi sort of put him in the mind of that actress Tasha Smith.

He was just about to bring his beer up to take a sip, as his eyes watched her across the room. When it seemed like something made her look his way and they made eye contact. Normally, he would have tried to play it off, but for some reason, he didn't, and he didn't look away either. Instead, Young Cas watched as she smiled, and even blew him a kiss.

Freak bitch, he thought. *Wanna play with niggaz emotions and shit.* He turned his head and sipped his beer.

$$$$

In New York, one of the common things to do, especially when you were high, was to go up and chill on the rooftop. That or ride the elevator down while you were on *TOP* of the elevator. All of this was shit niggaz did to boost their high. But Young Cas wasn't stupid, nor was he crazy. He wasn't about to ride no elevator down but he didn't have a problem chilling up on the roof. As long as they didn't expect him to do anything stupid, he was cool with it.

So, when Jameen and a couple of his boys left the party to do just that. Young Cas went with them. Now all three of them and him stood looking over the roof, out across Brooklyn. In the background, he could hear the *Camron* song *Welcome to New York City* playing.

"So, Prophet," One of the niggaz said. A nigga they called Hot. "Ya, lil nigga got his own set up now, huh?' He looked over at Young Cas.

"Yeah, yeah, "Jameen stated. "The nigga been doing good over in my trap. Decided it was time to get his own. I'm proud of the young nigga."

"But yo'," a nigga named Funk cut in. "What if niggaz step to ya lil' mans. Yo, can he hold it down?" he asked.

They waited while Jameen hit the cigarette he'd been smoking. At the same time, they could tell he was thinking about the question, too. Young Cas could hear the conversation, but he wasn't putting too much thought into it. In fact, he was still thinking about Papi and the way she'd been eyeballing him earlier. So, he didn't get to catch the rest of the conversation.

$$$$

He took a good long piss and then shook it off. Between the weed they smoked and the beers they drank. It seemed like all he wanted to do was piss or sleep.

Young Cas flushed the toilet and pulled the door open to step out of the bathroom. But when he stepped out into the hallway, he saw Papi leaning with her back against the wall, smoking a Newport. He stopped, she looked seductively like she was filming a cigarette commercial.

"So, what's up with you, lil' nigga?" Papi asked.

"I'm just trying to get my money right," he stated.

She inhaled, then blew the smoke out. "Tryna get yo' paper but no pussy?" she asked.

"What makes you say that?" Young Cas was confused. "Unless you're making an offer I don't know about." He watched as Papi smiled and hit the cigarette again. "There's a whole lot of pussy up in the party. I just didn't see you tryna fuck nothing. But hey, it ain't my business if you don't rock that way," she cracked.

Young Cas got the feeling that she was trying to be funny about it. "Nah, I just didn't think you rocked that way. Word is you like pussy, too. So, I assume you don't like dicks," he stated.

Young Cas watched. It seemed like she was thinking about something. Whatever it was, she appeared to be deep in thought about it.

"Maybe you just weren't feeling the nigga that was attached to the last dick you had," he suggested. "But hey, don't hold me responsible for that nigga."

$$$$

His every stroke was meticulously calculated, controlling both the depth and the speed by which he reached it. "Oh—oh shit—fuck, nigga—damn," she chanted almost as if she were auditioning for a role in the next porn movie to come out.

Young Cas had her lying across the bed, her thighs, and legs audaciously up across his shoulders. Both of his palms planted into the mattress as he leaned forward. His motions were so acute they were intense. His dick entered her pussy and stretched her out both in width and depth. Causing her walls to expand and extend inward to a deeper perpendicular abyss.

One that she didn't even know existed. Young made it a point to look into her eyes upon each inward stroke. She wouldn't have believed it even if one of God's Angels came down and told her that it was the truth. She knew that most of what he was doing to her was because she hadn't had anything larger than a finger inside of her body in some time. But she was surprise to see that it was this young nigga who was actually the one giving her the business.

Papi never would have thought this was at all possible. "Oh fuck," she said.

The sweat poured off both of their bodies. She had lost all track of time. Except for the fact that her joints were beginning to hurt. She couldn't say exactly how long they'd been at it in this one position. She assumed it had something to do with him drinking. That and him having been so young, but he was definitely standing up in the pussy. Young Cas didn't truly know what effect he was having on her.

All he knew was that she'd gone from liking dick. Having two kids, then became a dyke and no nigga seemed to be man enough to get into her stuff. So, since she gave him a shot at it. He intended to make it count and he did.

$$$$

"My name is Alexis, but I don't tell many people what it is," Papi stated.

After several rounds of sex, the sun was about to come up outside. They were lying back on the bed. He thought and listened while she smoked a Newport and talked. Already she'd told him why she became a dyke. A nigga having abused her sexually made her turn from men.

"I know one thing," Alexis continued. "I'll still like girls after tonight. But if yo' young ass ever comes through. And I ain't got nothing going on—" She blew the smoke out and glanced sideways. "We might be able to work something out."

He laughed before he said, "Girl, you, tripping. You and I both know that pussy belongs to Young Cas now. And I'ma get some whenever I decide to come through."

"You sho' is a cocky lil nigga ain't you?" she said but didn't deny anything he said.

"I'm just saying Prophet," Needle was in the process of saying. "I thought this was yo lil' mans in training and shit. But you want us to run up and test this niggaz gangsta?"

$$$$

At the moment the three of them were seated in the kitchen of an apartment. Jameen, Needle, and his partner Shakey. Both were junkies. Jameen for his own reasons did a lot of his slimy business with junkies.

"Yeah, I'm trying to see if this nigga been learning his lessons, "Jameen said. "And it's about time for the big test. The show and prove."

Needle looked over at Shakey both of them thinking the same thing. This nigga Prophet was on that bullshit again. This wasn't the first time Jameen had made a nigga in the streets and when the nigga got his weight up, he sent somebody at him. There was a saying in Brooklyn. *Jameen was the most crooked Prophet to ever exist. You wanna see a real snake, find Jameen, and hang around him. He'll definitely bite you.'*

So, they weren't surprised when Jameen came to them with this job. "Tell you what, Son," Shakey said. "We'll push up on yo' mans. But we keeping all the work. Shit, the nigga might try to stunt."

"Yeah, a'ight, "Jameen said. "But the nigga ain't got no heat. He just hustling off my face. So, no other niggaz ain't push up," he said.

Because the actual trap house that Young Cas was using had been one of his. The thing was the apartment wasn't making much money. He'd told Young Cas if he could buy a package and turn it in seven days. Then he would give him the trap. What he didn't know was that Young Cas had saved up enough loot to buy his first hook up of the boy. Or that Young Cas would learn how to cut his shit and mix it different, but he definitely doubled his shit in seven days.

That was nine weeks ago. Word just reached Jameen that this nigga was buying more weight from East New York, which meant Jameen could no longer tell what the nigga was moving. So, he assumed, from the math he'd done. That Young Cas was making something like four or five grand a week in the trap that had only yielded him a measly $1500.00 a week.

Jameen wasn't smelling that. Something about the shit wasn't right. He didn't want to lose his control over the young nigga. It had taken him too much work to get the young nigga in the first place. So, he needed to knock him down a few steps before he started thinking that he didn't need the Prophet.

$$$$

"You know that I knew your old lady?" Alexis said as she laid across the bed.

She watched as Young Cas got dressed to leave and as he paused pulling his jeans up. "Yeah?" Young Cas said. He really didn't like to talk about his mother. Because it usually brought back bad memories.

"Yeah, that nigga she was with, Coogi," Alexis told him. "He used to boost shit for Jameen. A few times they bought stuff over here and I helped them sell it. But Sonya was a nice one—" she paused. Young Cas sat on the edge of the bed to pull his Timberlands on. "I could tell she was getting in a bad way with that stuff. But in the hood, niggaz had to mind their own business," she explained.

Young Cas didn't see any problem with that. He knew and understood the code of the streets, and minding your own business was a big rule in New York. That and keep your eyes inside of your head and not in someone else's shit.

"A'ight so look, I'ma head back to my lab. So, when you want a nigga to come through?" he asked.

"I thought you just said this was your pussy now?" Alexis stated. "Don't that mean you don't need permission to come through?" she asked.

Young Cas looked back at her once he reached the door and was about to leave the apartment. "Don't play wit' me, girl. You know what's up," he stated then opened the door and stepped out.

It was only after he'd gone that Alexis laughed at him acting tough. She also wondered, just how much Young Cas knew about Jameen and the things he did?

$$$$

Young Cas caught a chill as he stepped out of the apartment building. He rubbed both of his hands together and blew warm air into them as he glanced first to the left, then to the right. Looking up both ends of the streets. He needed to head back to Flatbush where his trap house was over on Church Avenue. So, he turned and started walking because he would have to catch the train. He didn't have enough for a cab and didn't feel like making the long walk.

He looked both ways before he crossed the street and headed down the stairs to the subways. Upon entering the substation port, he paid and then made his way down to wait. While he stood there, he thought about his hustle thus far. He was doing good. Having made a couple of trips back out to Pink Houses and gotten the ugly nigga Jameen sent him to that time, to fuck with him. Ugly gave him a pretty good deal. He'd been able to spend $350.^{00} the first trip and made $800.^{00} which he reinvested and turned into $2000.^{00}. At the moment he was moving an ounce of crack cocaine.

Ugly kept stressing that he had some good boy he could fuck with him on. Young Cas had thought about it, fucking with heroin wasn't something he really wanted to do. Especially not with the shit that his moms went through. Jameen thought he was though.

The train came and he hopped on, made his way to the back, and took a seat. It wasn't really crowded at the moment. Then again, it was still early in the morning. As he sat back to enjoy the ride. The train hadn't started moving yet. He looked up when someone took the seat across from him. Young Cas found himself looking at the bum that was on the train that time he was with Jameen. The only difference was this guy wasn't dirty and bummy looking. Instead, he was clean and even wearing the latest fashion in gear. When he looked up into the man's eyes, Young Cas saw that he was smiling at him.

"Peace, God! How you be?" he asked. Leaving Young Cas vexed.

"Uh, peace," he stated.

He watched as the other man glanced around. "Yo' where's your Enlightener?" he asked.

"Who, Jameen?" Young Cas hunched his shoulders.

Then there was a pregnant pause between them. "A'ight," the guy said. "So, let me clear the present atmosphere. I come in the divine name of Unique Scientist Born Lord God Allah—" he paused to let that reality soak in. Then said, "I know they call you Young Castro. So, this kid Jameen ain't bless you wit' an identity other than that?" he asked.

"Nah, probably because I haven't officially become God Body," Young said. "But yo, I thought you was a homeless nigga and shit?" He watched as Unique smiled.

You went against the universal third law. It says to see things as they are, not how they appear to be. Do the knowledge, a wise man can play the role of a fool. However, a fool isn't intelligent enough to play the role of a wise man," he explained.

Young Cas remembered exactly what it said in his Supreme Alphabets. Then another thought came to his mind, so he spoke on it. "So, how come you were playing the role of a bum?" he asked.

"Good question, God," Unique stated. "The truth of the matter is, I've been watching this nigga Prophet. The Gods and Earths ain't exactly happy wit' the nigga and what he's got going on," he explained. "So—" He glanced around again before he continued. But there wasn't anyone sitting close enough to overhear their conversation. "I decided to look into the nigga. Get as close to his cipher as I could and see what was real. And then I observed him building with you that day," he said. Unique watched as a contemplative look came across Young Cas's face. He smiled. "Yeah, I'm talking about that day he hit you with that trick knowledge. But yo, a lot of shit niggaz gotta be able to see for themselves," Unique explained.

Young Cas already knew that. It was often referred to as self-savior. Meaning that a man would have to be able to save himself. No one else could be his savior. It was his responsibility, but then he thought about something else.

"Yo, how long you been watching Jameen?" he asked and watched Unique tilt his head in thought. "Not too long, I'd say about three months," Unique told him. Then added, "But I've been knowing the nigga like ten years. I'm from Medina, too."

Medina was what the Five Percenters called Brooklyn, they call Harlem Mecca. It was said that to them, Harlem was the heart of New York City. It was also the birthplace of the Five Percenters. What a lot of people outside of New York didn't know. Was that it was the Five Percenters that gave birth to a lot of New York's consciousness. They were even the pioneers of the Hip-Hop era.

Young Castro on the other hand was trying to figure out what was up with this nigga Unique. He could sense that there was something else going on, but he couldn't say what just yet.

Trai'Quan

Chapter Seven

Augusta, GA

Juggernaut made the sharp right turn and began to slow the Escalade down as he approached his destination. He was in North Augusta, S.C. Which wasn't a physical part of Augusta GA. It was actually named by its location and how close it was to Augusta, but it was still across the bridge. He also reached over and turned his music down as he began to enter the parking lot of Walmart. It was late, after 10:00 p.m., and even though Walmart was now a 24 Hour superstore. There weren't too many vehicles in the parking lot. He didn't care that it was the far end of the large parking lot where he saw the different rides. Most of them were SUVs, Denali's, Dodge Durangos, Expeditions, then there were a few Benzes and an old school Cutlass.

Juggernaut maneuvered and pulled up beside the Cream colored 4.6 HSE that Cream was pushing. He parked and stepped out. When he looked around, he took note of all who were present. Ace, Cream, Poe, and his partner Tech 9. Then standing in front of the Denali were Young Castro and Jeeta. Juggernaut bobbed his head at all of them.

$$$$

It was Jeeta who pushed off the front of the Denali and made a small circle to look at each one of them. He already had his instructions, so he knew what Young Castro expected of him.

I'm glad all of you could show up—" He paused to look at Juggernaut. "Be mindful, this may not be a white-collar board room meeting, but it's still an exclusive event. Meaning

63

punctuality is necessary." He watched as Juggernaut nodded acknowledgment. Everyone else followed his example. Jeeta waited long enough to be sure that he was understood clearly. Even though he was older than Young Castro. He knew that to be successful they needed to move with precision. Every step had to be well calculated and strategically executed.

"Alright, here's what's going on," Jeeta began. "Ace, you and Juggernaut have both been officially accepted into the fold. However, the consequences and repercussions for failure are extremely high. We don't have room for mistakes. So, if your head ain't in this game. Then put it out there so we can go ahead and deal with it," he explained clearly.

He waited, giving anyone the opportunity to say something if they needed to, but no one spoke or even glanced his way.

$$\$\$\$\$$

Young Castro leaned back onto the Denali, listening as Jeeta delivered the rules and regulations to them. He couldn't help but reflect over his life. All the things that made him what he was today. Every good, that he received and the bad, he'd lived through. He thought about that business he'd left unfinished back in Brooklyn. That within itself was something he knew he would have to deal with one day. No matter how many times he postponed it. The reality was it had to be taken care of.

$$\$\$\$\$$

"Money Loc, what's going on?" Hernandez asked. Having just walked up to the table where the four Crips sat inside

Cloud 9, a club that was located in Daniel Village Plaza, off Wrightsboro Road.

Cloud 9 was hot right now. In fact, it was the hottest club except for the Caribbean style club over in Southgate Plaza, owned by the Jamaican. The atmosphere inside Cloud 9 was nice and there were a lot of single ladies moving about.

"What's crackin', cuz? "Money Loc lifted halfway up in his seat and pushed his hand out to shake the large Mexican's hand.

Hernandez stood well over 6'4 and had that massive bulky build like any other Mexican with some size on him. He was a powerful figure in Mara Salvatruda or as most people knew it as MC-13. Since they also wore the color blue it was kind of like a mutual respect thing between them and the Crips.

As he stood there, Hernandez looked around the table at Money Loc's boys. Two of them he knew, C-Loc and Tru-Loc.

"Oh, my bad, cuz." Money Loc saw the confusion on the other man's face. "This my nigga, Lil' Snoop and that's Jay-Loc," he introduced the two, who threw their C's up. "So, what's on your mind, cuz? You still beefing with that nigga Jeeta?" Money Loc asked.

Hernandez smirked. "I don't do beefing," Hernandez stated. For a thirty-eight-year-old, he sounded surprisingly younger. "Whenever a problem I have gets out of the way, I get out of the way. And watch as the Sicario come through. But that's not what I wanted to see you about. You mind?" Hernandez spoke to C-Loc. Who scooted closer to Jay-Loc so that Hernandez could squeeze in to sit down. Once he was seated, he looked across at Money Loc. "Tell me what you know about these bitches on twenty-third?" he asked, giving Money-Loc his undivided attention.

He watched as Money Loc whistled. "You talking about the Blaylock girls?" Money Loc gave names to them. He paused a moment in thought. As if he were trying to figure out how to explain them. "Listen, cuz, this is some real shit. So, don't take none of it lightly, a'ight?" he stated and watched as Hernandez nodded for him to continue. Still focused on every word. "There's like four of them. All of them are some bad bitches. It's all centered around the mother. Her name is Trish. And she might just be the toughest bitch I ever heard of," Money Loc explained. "The rumor is that they're all from Philly. Up there Trish was some type of prostitute. Not the kind with a pimp. But the bitch sold pussy. She's seen the rough side of life. All three of her daughters have the same father. But that ain't what makes her a bad bitch—" He fell quiet for a moment and reached for his glass so he could sip his drink.

Money Loc kind of suspected that Hernandez was looking to expand his operation. If he was thinking about expanding out to Hepzibah, out to Travis Pine and Farington, then the Crips wouldn't be a part of that move. Not many crews would.

"So, tell me, what makes this Chola tough?" Hernandez asked.

"Let's see, "Money Loc began. "Trish came to Augusta sometime in the nineties. I can't get the exact date right. But what I do know is she started fucking wit this nigga T.J., Terry Johnson. A big dope boy out of Florida somewhere. Anyway, she's fuckin' with this nigga. And at the time all her girls were young. All of them were under seventeen then. Well, the story goes this nigga T.J. must've gotten his hands on some bad dope. He had to be high, trying one of them young girls—" He paused and sipped his drink. "They say when Trish woke up. Having heard the scream. She went to the room and found this big black ass nigga trying to force himself on her baby.

And she snapped, a whole.357 snap at that. She wacked the nigga with his own shit. But that ain't even what made her a bad bitch," Money Loc said.

He saw that he held Hernandez's undivided attention. He wasn't sure how much of this the Mexican had already heard and was trying to check and see if it was real. He knew Hernandez had heard something. Trish Blaylock and her girls were in a bad situation out in Hephzibah.

"What made her a bad bitch?" Hernandez asked.

"This nigga T.J. was originally from Haiti. So, he was an Island boy. After Trish killed him, she had enough sense to move all the dope out of the house before she called the cops. They arrested her, but not for the murder. They called that a crime of passion. They took her to jail because the .357 was hot and had been used in the murder of some other niggaz in Augusta a year earlier. So, they had to arrest her. But they let her out.

They figured the nigga T.J. was the one that killed them. Which was actually an old case. One where the DEA were raiding Butler Manner and a shootout started. Everyone seemed to have forgotten that there had been a lot of Haitians in Butler Manner when all that went down. Everyone became focused on the people that died that day. What happened was," Money Loc said.

"Some island boys came up from Florida. They were under the impression that someone had robbed and killed this nigga T.J. They were saying he had over twenty-five kilos of coke when he died and they wanted blood. So, they rode around Augusta for approximately five days making threats. Mind you, this bitch wasn't from Augusta. So, she didn't have any family to turn to for protection."

Hernandez seemed to be all into the story now. "So, what happened?" he asked.

"Well, they never really tell this part clearly. They make it out like a fuckin movie or something," Money Loc said. "Word is the island boys were all piled up in a four-door Chevy Blazer. And pulled up to a stoplight. They say all of them were smoking weed. So, they were pretty high at the time—" He paused. "The Blazer was behind a school bus," he continued.

"It's said that one of Trish's daughters was driving when they pulled the Suburban up behind the Blazer boxing it in. Trish along with two of her other girls exited the truck in all black, holding a Mack 11, Uzi-9mm and she had an AK-47 herself. They say the three of them walked up alongside the Blazer and lit that muthafucka up." Money Loc laughed. "And I forgot the shit happened right about 4:30 p.m. They say she'd just picked her girls up from school," he finished then turned his drink up.

He was giving the Mexican enough time to think over what he'd said. "So, listen cuz, "he continued. "Since then, the bitch has flipped that dope a hundred times. And it's just her and her girls out there. And they've got them LOE niggaz backing them. Her next to the oldest girl Sabrina. She has a son and a daughter by one of them niggaz. You might have even heard of him. The nigga named Trigger. Tall, brown-skinned nigga originally from Sunset. So, if you push up on them bitchez. Them LOE Life niggas gon' get involved.

This is why the Crips weren't about to get into that one. They knew what happened the last time somebody went after the Blaylock girls. A group of Bloods who had to be stupid. They didn't have enough sense to kill them when they had them down bad. Just like some frontin ass niggaz. While they had all four of the Blaylock girls pent down in a shootout. The niggaz took time to talk shit, brag about it. While they were doing that. Sabrina was calling her baby's daddy on her iPhone. Five minutes later, twelve carloads of niggaz pulled up into Farington. A whole lot of Bloods, bled that day. Nowadays, the Bloods weren't allowed in Farington or Travis Pine. Because there were some LOE niggaz out there now.

$$$$

Hernandez left the club and got into his Range Rover Sport. He'd listen to the story that Money Loc told and while he was sure the first part was true. He just couldn't see a family of four women being that strong. Oh, he knew they had the work. He'd found out that they were buying coke from one of Jeeta's crew. Some fool named Cream. Who was also doing his thing out of Governor's Place. There was a rumor of him moving weight in a few other spots throughout Augusta, too. How much exactly, he couldn't really say.

Hernandez didn't know if he was fucking with one of them or not. But he really didn't care. His mind was focused on the area. Because at the moment his empire was growing, and Central Ave wasn't big enough to hold it all. His sister had something going on with the dope boys in Harrisburg, but even that wasn't enough. He still had too much product coming in and it was coming in fast.

He had one of two choices. He could make a move on these bitches on 23rd. Or he could go up against the Animals. That's what Jeeta's crew were calling themselves, the Animals. Where they hustled was the Jungles. It almost didn't make sense. Ginning Holmes was Jungle 4, Sunset Villa was Jungle 2. Pinewalk was Jungle 6 and so on and so forth. Wherever they controlled the area it was called a Jungle. Then a number.

From what people were telling him. These guys were acting like real animals. So, Hernandez figured, these

Blaylock bitches might be the lesser of two evils. If he went after them and got all of them before the LOE Life guys showed up. He might be in the good. Yet and still, he was going to think about it some more. Wasn't no sense in making a foolish mistake.

Chapter Eight

"These bitches think I'm something to play with," Diane made the statement while sitting in front of the gas station's parking lot.

At the moment, she was sitting behind the wheel of the black on black, 2008 Navigator that she'd dropped a few stacks on. This being the latest of her work vehicles. The GMC Blazer she used to use had gotten too hot, she suspected the cops had a good description of it.

"The niggaz act like I'm pussy or something. Somebody help me out here. Do I look like I'm pussy?" she asked.

Over in the passenger seat, Sabrina gazed out the windshield to where two niggaz were hustling. The nigga that Diane said owed her money. Then she looked over to where her older sister sat. In her hand, she was gripping the latest edition 9mm Desert Eagle. On the other hand, she fiddled with the extra clip.

"Nah, bitch, you might be sexy, but not at all soft and wet like pussy," 'Brina said she spoke with a slight Northern accent. Mostly because she'd spent so much time in Germantown, North Philly while growing up.

'Brina took in the Seven jeans that looked like they had been melted onto Diane. She also wore an all-black Coogi sweater, with the black Timberland Euro boots that came with the bubble gum soles. At the moment, though all three of them were dressed alike.

"Nessa, do I look pussy to you?" Diane asked looking up into the rearview at the other woman, who was in the back seat of the SUV.

"Nah, bitch, I can't see your pussy from back here." Vanessa paused in feeding shells into the pistol grip pump that she held. She was the baby of the family.

"Hmm, hmm I thought so," Diane stated. "You bitches ready to put this work in or what?"

To which Sabrina laughed. "Gurl, I feel like a virgin on prom night. Pussy all wet and shit."

"Me too my fucking jeans are all wet and shit," Vanessa added from the back seat. "The damn things are so tight I'm about to bust a nut just holding this pump."

"A'ight then let's get this money." Diane started the truck and put it in gear.

$$$$

"Nigga—fuck Diane—fuckin' D-block bitch don't scare no grown-ass man," Big Chief made the statement as if it truly did come from his heart.

He was sick and tired of Boogie Man constantly bringing up the fact that they hadn't paid her the money that they owed. It was mostly because she'd only asked about it once, and that was over the phone. That was a few weeks ago. Right now, they were about to run out of product. Which meant that if they couldn't re-up with her. They would have to find another pipeline. At the moment, the other weight boy's prices were higher than those Diane had.

"Yeah, nigga, I feel you, but—" Boogie man stated. "It's not out of fear that I brought the issue up. Nigga we got a business to run, Po' bitch and we can't do that if a nigga ain't got shit to sell," he explained.

Big Chief thought about it. He knew Boogie Man was right. But at the same time, he kept thinking about how this bitch would pull up, stressing that D-Block shit. Acting like she don't bleed once a month, and that she just gave birth to Jesus Christ or some shit. So, even if he did have a few bands to pay her. He felt like the bitch owed him some fuckin' respect. Fuck D-Block, he was one of the toughest niggaz in Augusta, right now. All the other tough niggaz were in prison or graveyards.

"Fuck it, thug. What's done is done," he stated. "The bitch ain't been down here to the bottom yet. Maybe she done charged it to the game. But look we might have to holla at that nigga Juggernot."

Boogie Man wasn't so sure about that. He damn sure didn't think going up to 12th Street to buy weight was a good idea. Niggaz on 12th and O-S, *Old Savannah Road* didn't fuck with niggaz from the bottom like that. You really had to know somebody like that to get some real fucking with.

$$$$

Trapp-Loc thought *These niggaz had to be stupid.* He was wondering if they knew that they were playing with fire. At the moment, he was leaning back onto the hood of his Lexus LS 400 waiting on one of his boys to come back out of the apartment they trapped out of. He'd gone inside to get the load. Trapp-Loc's eyes were observing both Big Chief and Boogie Man as they hustled. Most people down here in Allen Holmes knew that they'd been grinding for D-Block. Nearly everybody knew that they owed her some money.

What they might not know was that Diane, a.k.a Diane Blaylock B.K.A to the streets, D-Block. Didn't forgive and she damn sure didn't forget. Trapp-Loc was hustling over on 23rd, and he used to work for the nigga who had it before the Blaylock girls. That nigga came up missing. Some said the Feds got him. Others speculated that the Blaylock girls did. Nobody seems to know for sure, but he knew about D-Block firsthand and how she moved on Travis Pine.

He also knew that if she didn't come through. Then her son's father and his partner would definitely show up. This nigga Damian wasn't even a dope boy. In fact, nobody knew what he did. Other than the fact that he was younger than D-Block and would see about any nigga who violated her. Baby mama drama for real.

Trapp-Loc was in the process of taking a pull on the Newport he was smoking and completing that thought when the black SUV with the too dark tint on its windows pulled up. The truck, for some reason he couldn't fathom, pulled up right next to his Lexus with its music playing.

Ooohhh, mercy, mercy me/Things ain't what they used to be/oh mercy mercy, meeee.

The music was pumping hard out of the truck. For some strange reason, he had a bad feeling about it. Then the driver's side window cracked just enough for the driver to speak.

"Hey, playboy you got a gram of that white girl?" The female voice called out.

Trapp-Loc froze. Because it suddenly seemed as if he was on a movie set and the director had just yelled. "Action!"

$$$$

Boogie Man knew that this sale was for them. Because Trapp-Loc didn't make sales himself, and none of his boys were on deck at the moment. Besides, very few people sold power cocaine in their projects. Since Big Chief was standing over near one of the apartment complexes taking a piss with his back to the streets. He decided to go ahead and make this sell himself.

He pushed his right hand down into his pants pocket for the plastic baggies as he turned to the truck, but he wasn't paying close attention. So, when he finally pulled the cocaine out and looked up, his reality all of a sudden changed. The driver's side door came open and Diane jumped out with her gun in her hand. At the same time the passenger side door opened. Boogie Man's jaw fell to the ground.

"What's up nigga, D-Block?"

"Oh shit!" He turned, and all 6'2 and 213lb of him struck out in a sprint like he was an Atlanta Brave making a dash for home plate in the world series.

$$$$

Big Chief had only just gotten about half of the urination out of his body. As a result of all the Coronas, he'd put away earlier. Then he heard Boogie Man curse. At first, he thought it was the *Jump Out Boys*, the cops. When he took the chance to glance back. He saw Diane as she leaned forward and set out at a run. Followed by one of her sisters, both of them holding guns. He pissed on himself as he too broke out running. His pants were wet, and his dick still hung out of the zipper slot.

$$$$

"You get fat boy, I've got tall and sexy," Diane called out as she ran. Both of them were about the same height and build, but Big Chief was slightly larger in the belly.

$$$$

Sabrina, the tallest of the trio, didn't hesitate. She'd already been in motion with her twin .45s swinging by her side. Her grip tight on both. There wasn't any need for extra wordplay. They both knew what to do. This wasn't the first time they'd had to ride on some stupid ass niggaz.

Trapp-Loc couldn't really believe what he was seeing. Here it was, not quite 6:00 p.m. and these two crazy bitches were chasing these niggaz with guns out. On top of all that, he couldn't take his eyes off those fat asses jiggling in those tight jeans. In fact, he was so distracted that he didn't hear the back door of the Navigator open. His head froze in place when he heard the noise.

Kah! Chic!

"Eye's up, daddy. This ain't no peep show," Vanessa stated as she sat facing out of the back seat with the door open and the pump aimed at Trapp Loc's back.

The music was still playing in the background. Almost like it was being filmed. Diane had told them that only the two niggaz she pointed out were to get it, but if anybody else got into their business, then whatever. Nessa was hoping this nigga built his nuts up to act stupid. Because she was horny as fuck and dying to shoot somebody.

$$$$

Diane wasn't about to run a marathon with this nigga. As she closed some of the distance between him and her. She brought her 9mm up and squeezed off four shots. The first two hit him in the shoulder and center of his back. While the last two hit him in the ass and back of his left thigh. She slowed her pace when she saw his body pitch face-first into the sidewalk.

Walking calmly now, she approached the spot where Boogie Man still groped and tried to crawl. She didn't even hesitate. Diane delivered two more slugs to the back of his head. Then she heard Sabrina's cannons.

$$$$

Having aimed at both of his legs because Big Chief was a large guy. At 6'3 he had to be close to 300lbs. So, Sabrina took both of his legs away from him. Sending him to the ground screaming like a bitch. By the time she walked up and stood over him. She heard Diane running toward her.

"Oh—oh—somebody help me! Please don't let these crazy bitches kill me!"

"Nigga you ain't seen a crazy bitch yet, "Diane stated as she came to stand next to Sabrina. "Where my fuckin' money at nigga?"

"Oh, shit—s—some of it—I—" They watched as Big Chief rolled to the side and reached into his pocket.

At that time, Sabrina turned and walked back to the truck. She jumped into the driver's seat and backed up just as Diane snatched the two rolls of bills out of his hands.

"Soft ass, nigga." She looked at the money. "This ain't nowhere near what you owe me, but it's all good."

She aimed the 9mm and pulled the trigger, putting two slugs in his face. She turned and looked back at Trapp-Loc and the other dope boys who were all standing around watching.

"D-Block! What?" She held her gun up. "You niggaz look like you wanna be some witnesses?" Everyone, including Trapp-Loc, threw their hands up to the sky. In the distance, she could hear the police sirens.

"Bitch," Vanessa called out. "If you done advertising yo' brand, you can get yo' hot ass in this truck."

Diane ran around to the passenger's side door which was still open. She jumped in just as Sabrina pressed the gas and pull off.

"Slow the fuck down girl," Diane said as she leaned sideways with the truck's movement.

About a mile away from the projects they bypassed two police cars headed in the opposite direction. In the backseat, Vanessa fired up a thick stick of some good that she'd rolled in tonfan leaf. She actually rolled that before they went to do the job. Vanessa took several tokes and coughed. Then passed it.

"What's up, girl? You good? "Diane asked.

"Nah, I think I got a nut just then. I need to get out of these jeans. Shit."

Diane shook her head. Because she'd just had her second child 2 ½ months ago. She knew Damian would be pissed if he knew she was out in the streets, but their bloodline really originated in Trinidad. Meaning that they all had that island blood in them. So, they didn't move like most black women.

Lake Almstead apartments sat at the top of Broad Street. It was next to the Savannah River, there was also a park and boating area. Over the years it gained some fame, starting back when a dope boy named Randy trapped out of it. Randy was doing Fed time these days and Lake Almstead apartments were being hustled by a group of Mexicans and some Crips.

At the moment C-Loc was sitting on the hood of his old school 1965 Impala with a candy paint job on it that was deep blue. The ride also had some nice rims and a hydraulic system that he'd just had installed. C-Loc sat there parked in front of his girl's apartment, talking on his phone. He glanced up when the black Avalanche pulled up behind his ride and Tru-Loc jumped out. C-Loc finished up his conversation and shared a fist bump with Tru-Loc.

"What's crackin', cuz?" C-Loc asked.

"Just got word from Money. He said we're good with the Mexicans on that next drop," Tru-Loc said.

"Good cause we really need that. Especially with this nigga Jetta over in Harrisburg. The nigga doing some big numbers from what I've heard," C-Loc explained.

Somehow and no one could say exactly, but Jeeta seemed to have an endless supply of work. Added with the GBI putting the press down lately. A hustler had to be smart. They'd already put away several of the known names. No one knew who else they had on that list, but Jetta was still moving his shit.

"I'll be glad when this thing between him and these Mexicans blow up," Tru-Loc stated.

"Fo' sho', cuz. Let them fools kill each other while we stay out here getting money." C-Loc laughed.

They both knew that Money-Loc was in the process of pitting Jeeta against Hernandez. If that worked, the two of them would get rid of each other or destroy their business in a war. While in the background they would be left to pick up the pieces.

$$$$

Money-Loc whipped his ride in and out of traffic. Loving the feel of it as he drove the new Expedition. He was just thinking of how nice the truck handled when his phone vibrated.

"Yooo," he answered.

"What's crackin', cuz? I thought you were coming through. We gotta meet wit' yo' boy, right?" Jay-Loc asked.

"Yeah, yeah. That's still blue, I'm almost to your crib now." Money-Loc made another turn. "As a matter of fact, I'm pulling into your spot now."

Jay-Loc lived with a girl named Keisha that he had a daughter with. They lived in Fox den which also happened to be one of Jay-Loc's trap spots. Money-Loc pulled the Expedition up next to Jay-Loc's Suburban.

"I see you, cuz," Jay-Loc said as he pulled the curtain aside to look out of window. "I'm on my way out now," he stated.

Money-Loc sat there waiting. Listening to a song by Young Jeezy and Gucci Mane. It didn't take that long for Jay-Loc to exit the apartment. In one hand he carried a Champion gym bag. Money-Loc already knew that it held his half of the money needed for this deal. He was already on the back seat. Jay opened the passenger side door and got in.

"Let's go get it, cuz." He laughed.

Money-Loc backed out of the parking space. They were meeting with Hernandez and his partner, his sister Juanita. On this deal, they were buying 5 kilos which they would split two ways. Over the past year, it seemed like the Feds had an inside man. Because they took down nearly all the major players. A couple was able to bounce back. Like Juggernaut and Ace, while some managed to wag like Jeeta and those bitches up in Hephzibah.

Money-Loc simply couldn't see them buying from Jeeta. That in turn would be them buying from them New York niggaz, Young Castro and Poe. He knew what was going on. It was being played to look like Jeeta was his own man. Where in, Money -Loc could remember that Jeeta had never moved weight until he started fucking with the nigga Young Castro. They knew he had his hands in a bigger pot. So, that meant Jeeta was working for this nigga. Or the nigga was giving Jeeta a damn good deal on the product. Enough that Jeeta could push weight and look like he was the man.

Chapter Nine

"Okay, okay listen, Pah," Young Castro interrupted as Cream and Poe argued.

Jeeta sat at the table quietly listening. The topic had been the Blaylock girls and them running around shooting shit up like they were on some Wild West Cowboys shit. Poe was saying they were bad for business. Cream was saying they weren't going to let niggaz just disrespect them.

Their meeting was taking place inside California Dream, a nice restaurant on Washington Road. This was one of those meetings that Young Castro called when they had a situation. Right now, the Blaylock girls were in a situation. Because they were doing business with them. Some of the other businesspeople knew that and were worried.

"Cream, you go talk to your girl," Young Castro stated. "Tell her they need to take it down a notch. Yo' Pah, I know you and Shorty cool and shit, but this is business, Son. What they do, can affect everybody," he explained.

Cream nodded his head, the relationship between him and Vanessa Blaylock was kind of funny. They hadn't gotten physical or anything, but there was definitely an attraction there. Vanessa on the other hand was still somewhat involved with her son's father.

"I got it, son," Cream said.

"But listen, Pah." Young Castro added. "Explain to them that I'm not telling them to be soft and not handle their business. Shit, that's why we're in business with them in the first place. But the next time they got a problem. They need to check-in. Let niggaz know they about to go kill niggaz," he said.

"Especially if it can cause a war. "Jeeta added.

Because Trapp-Loc was one of his people and while he didn't have any hard feelings about Vanessa holding a gun on him. He still felt disrespected.

"Tell her there ain't no beef, but she needs to be mindful about who she points her gun at," Jeeta said.

"A'ight, a'ight, I'ma pull-up," Cream stated.

Their deal had actually been established between Young Castro and the mother Trish Blaylock. Her having received word that Young Castro was the one she needed to see in order to purchase weight. After Mishna had been hit by the GBI and hadn't been able to sell her the weight he promised. She'd been looking for a more permanent source. So, she came to Young Castro and they made a deal. He was able to sell her ten bricks at thirty grand cheaper than anyone else would have. Trish felt that was a blessing, especially when she realized that it was the same price every time she brought from him. That made it easier for her to get product without having to drive to Miami and back.

Then Cream met Vanessa, the baby girl at one of the drop-offs and they started vibing somewhat. It would have been easier for Young Castro to go see Trish about her daughters, but they would think Trish was trying to punish them. Then they would rebel, especially D-Block. That one they all knew wouldn't listen. Then again Young Castro could have pushed up on Damian and asked him to control his baby's mother, but Young Castro respected Damian and didn't want any bad blood between them. So, it would have to be Cream that delivered the message to them. Besides, he liked the way they did business.

$$$$

"Damn that's them kids Big Chief and Boogie Man right there. Ayo, I thought they worked for your Earth, Son?"

Justice glanced over to where Damian sat in the recliner watching TV. He brought the Heineken up and took a sip. Justice was wondering if Damian was the one that killed the two dope boys. The cops were saying they were killed in broad daylight but no one in Allen Holmes was willing to ID the shooter or shooters.

"The fuck you lookin' at me like that for?" Damian asked.

Justice chuckled and pulled out a blunt. He also whipped out a lighter and put fire to it. After taking a few drags he passed it. "Yeah, a'ight," Justice mumbled. "Let me find out, Son. Let me find out," he said with a deep New York accent. "I heard them kids thought they had all the noodles. Niggaz said they'd tried a few niggaz way back."

"Yeah." Damian tried to keep the smoke deep inside of his lungs as he passed the blunt back.

Both of them were originally from Queensbridge but had been in the south now for the past five years. Damian having been with Diane the past three. Their son Nike was approaching his second birthday. It wasn't exactly a secret that Diane was touching a few bricks. Most people assumed that Damian had his hand in it, but he didn't. Neither he nor Justice even sold dope.

"They probably should have kept trying niggaz," Damian mumbled causing Justice to shoot him a crooked eye.

"Yeah, yeah let a nigga find out. Have heads back home thinkin' we down here on some—" Justice paused to hit the blunt again. "Down here on some Kevin Costner bodyguard shit."

He continued talking but Damian shook his head. Justice often had a tendency to ramble. Damian suspected that Justice thought he'd been the one to body the two flakes, but he hadn't. Even though bodywork really was his M.O. That's what he and Justice did. However, most of their work was done on calls that came from the Boss. Justice should know they hadn't received a call in a minute. Damian didn't get involved in Diane's business. Unless she had a problem she really couldn't solve. He knew that D-Block could solve most of her own problems. He only felt some kind of way because she'd just had their daughter and wasn't supposed to be in the streets. Damian still felt like it was reckless for her to be putting in her own work. But the Boss had given him strict instructions not to get in the way of Young Castro's operation. And the Blaylock girls were definitely a part of his operation.

As he hit the blunt Damian was aware that Justice was still looking at him speculatively. "What nigga," he asked.

"Let a nigga find out," Justice mumbled. But Damian ignored it. Justice was under the impression that D-Block didn't really do all of her own bodywork. He thought Damian was responsible for some of it. There had been one or two situations where he'd come through about his baby's momma. But it wasn't on a regular. D-Block could handle her own.

$$$$

"Who the fuck is this blowing up my damn phone?" Vanessa said in frustration as she walked into her living room to find her phone. It had been ringing for a minute, but she had to see about her daughter Toiya who was only five. When she found the phone and looked at the number. Instead of being mad, Vanessa smiled. "Uh oh, my boo thang," she said to herself before answering the call. "Hey, what's up with you?" she asked.

"Not much but I need to see you," Cream said. "Is your nigga around?"

"Nah, that nigga in the streets. What's on your mind?"

There was a short pause. "My mans wanted me to pull up on ya about that business that's being talked about in the streets. It almost caused some waves," he said.

"Yeah, D-Block been on the bullshit. So, what's up, you coming through a what?" she asked.

"You already know I'm not gonna come up to your spot. I'd hate to bump heads with your man. That ain't gonna be good for nobody," Cream explained. "Snatch your little girl up and meet me at Cheddas in like forty-five minutes."

She looked at the time on her red-gold Dior watch with twenty-four small diamonds in it. "Okay, I'll meet you there." She ended the call.

$$$$

Cream looked up when he saw her walk in. Like every other time he saw her, he was stuck on stupid. Vanessa Blaylock wasn't exactly your black woman *thick in the hips type*. Instead, as he watched her and the little girl with her approached the table, Cream took in all of her. She was wearing an expensive dress by Versace that reached mid-thigh and two-inch Giuseppe heels.

Vanessa wasn't thick fine, she was petite fine. Her 6'0 frame was only 150lbs and toned from exercise. Her figure would be around 33-24-34 he knew her ass wasn't super big, but it was a nice handful, and the damn girl was just beautiful. She was a dark-brown skin and had long natural eyelashes. Her eyes were the sleepy kind that made a man want to spend time looking into them.

Cream stood to greet them as they reached his table. "I get to spend this time with two beautiful ladies, huh?" he cracked. Then helped Toiya into her seat and held the seat for

Vanessa. "So, what do you want to eat?" he asked and waved one of the waiters over to take their orders.

Once that was done, the food was brought. While Toiya ate, he turned to the reason he asked her to meet him.

"So, D-Block had to straighten her business, huh?" he asked.

"Yeah, you know D. She gets extreme at times," Vanessa said as she both ate and looked across the table into his eyes. "Young Castro must be upset about something?"

"Not really upset," Cream said. "Who drew down on the nigga in the Lexus?" he asked and saw her smile. He'd already known, he was just making sure.

"Oh, that was me. Why he important?" she asked.

"He's one of Jeeta's Crips, but he is part of the structure," Cream explained. "He really didn't appreciate being put in the middle of D-Block's business."

"If the nigga had kept his eyes in his head and not been lusting. He wouldn't have had that problem," Vanessa told him. "But I'm grown. I can accept my wrongs. So, what does Young Castro want us to do?"

"He's not asking y'all not to do your thing." Cream looked deep into her eyes as he spoke. While they sat there he still couldn't understand why she was with this nigga Rook. He was a dope boy and had some points in the streets, but the nigga was running around on her with two other girls that he had kids with and Vanessa knew it. He knew that she'd known because she told him about it. "Bruh, just need y'all to be a little more professional about it," he continued. "And a lot less noisy. He says you're part of our family now. And as a family if you have a problem, then we have a problem," he told her.

Vanessa continued eating her food as she listened. Then she asked. "So, what does he want us to do? Call one of you every time we have a problem and let y'all come handle it?"

she stated. "That's not gonna happen. We earned our respect by doing what we do. And we don't need a protection plan. That's what niggaz get GEICO for."

Cream was quiet, trying to figure out how to explain it to her. "Listen, love," he started and saw her smile. "It's not a protection plan. Bruh just feels like y'all need to give us a heads up when y'all put in work. Just in case something goes wrong. What if you find yourself in a tight situation? And Trigger or Damian can't get there in time, then what?" he asked and watched as she considered his words. "You think your boy Rook gon' come through?" he asked.

Vanessa sucked her teeth as she brushed that off. "So, what your saying is," she began. "You're prepared to be my back up. The way Damian will back D-Block or Trigger will back Brina?" she stated.

Vanessa smiled again; this smile was a seductive one. She was looking straight at him. Cream wasn't about to feed into it too much. They'd been doing this flirting thing for a while now and he still hadn't gotten close to having sex with her.

$$$$

"You know, Pah," Young Castro began. "Sometimes, I feel like I'm an old soul." He held the blunt up close to his face and looked at it closely. Over in the driver's seat, Jeeta was focused on watching the street as he drove, but he was still listening as Young Castro spoke. "It almost seems like I've been on this Earth a whole fucking lifetime, Pah. Like I watched the universe being created. Now that's some deep shit right there, Son. Deep shit," Young Castro said. Then he passed the blunt to Jeeta.

For a moment he sat there gazing out of the windshield. Mentally, he was thinking about Jameen and Alexis. He thought about Unique and all that he'd learned from him. Young Castro knew that he was high and that these were only memories. At the moment, he was in a good place. Then they saw the blue lights.

$$$$

DWB, That's what Young Castro was thinking after the white woman fingerprinted them, driving while black. The cops that pulled them over never said why they made the stop. Once Jetta pulled over, they made a big deal about the weed smoke which wouldn't have been a problem. Until they used it as probable cause and searched the truck. That's how they found the two guns, both of which had filed off serial numbers. That meant that they were either hot guns or had been used in a crime. Either way, the guns got them booked.

"Alright who's ready for their phone call?" the female booking officer asked.

Young Castro stood up and walked out of the holding cell to follow her to the phones. He lifted one of the receivers and punched in a number.

"Hello?" the female voice said.

"Ms. Alexandria—this is Casey Porter. Me and one of my friends were arrested tonight. The cops pulled us over and found two guns in the ride," he said.

"Okay, so you're at Phinizy Road then?" she asked.

"Yes, ma'am, me and a friend. They haven't given us a bond or fine yet," he explained.

"Don't worry about it, I'll take care of everything." She ended the call.

Diane Alexandra looked over at her husband who was still asleep. She glanced at the clock, it read 1:36 a.m. If she tried to call the jail now, she wouldn't get any real answers. If this was about the guns found in the car, then she'd have to speak with Agent Westson on the ATF. That would all have to be done around 9:00. So, she thought she might as well get some more rest.

$$$$

Unbeknownst to either Diane Alexandria or Casey Porter. At the same time, ATF Agent Sean Westson was sitting inside of a conference room. Across from him sat DEA Agent Mark Hamon. Both were senior agents and had quite a few years under their belts. They even knew one another casually. However, this meeting was business-related.

"So, how do want to go about it?" Sean Westson asked.

He looked down at the file that laid on the table. The folder contained a detailed report of a murder case involving five victims. One of which happened to be an ATF undercover agent. The investigation had been of some military guys that were selling guns stolen from the military armory. The guns were reported lost overseas and the paperwork was rewritten to show that the said guns hadn't re-entered the United States.

"Both of these guys are drug dealers," DEA agent Mark Hamon stated. "I have files on both of them that go back ways. They may be killers, too. But I don't think they'd have killed some white men and kept the guns."

Sean Westson gave that some thought. Truthfully, it didn't make much sense. "Unless they're low-level drug dealers and this was an actual robbery," he suggested.

Because no one knew what was missing from the murder scene. All the bodies had been stripped naked. Even the wire his guy wore, was gone. No doubt whoever committed the crime knew an undercover officer was killed and intended to conceal that fact.

"Oh, they're not," Mark Hamon stated. "Trust me when I say, these two guys are knee-deep into the drug game. Especially the one Casey Porter. In the streets, he's known as Young Castro."

"Well, maybe our guys were also conducting a drug deal as well," Westson suggested.

"Doesn't fit Castro's M.O.," Hamon said. "This guy, he's young, but not foolish. In fact, I don't think he would even show up to drug deals anymore. Which is one of the reasons it's becoming too hard to bust him. We can take down a few of his people. But we won't be able to get him or his partner, James Lomax. That's the one that's called Jeeta-Loc," he explained.

Westson thought about it. Initially, they knew at the ATF that the guns weren't missing. They had made it back to the U.S. After recovering several in a crime that happened in Dade County, Florida, they suspected these guns were being sold in the streets and these were some pretty high-end guns. They were the kind that the Federal Government didn't want in the streets. Especially in the hands of drug dealers.

"So, if the guys didn't commit the murders. Then maybe they know who did. Maybe whoever did it was the one to sell them the guns," Weston suggested.

"That seems more possible than them doing it. But I don't think they'll talk," Hamon told him.

"If we scare them with—" Westson started.

Hamon started shaking his head. "Won't work," he said. "This guy Castro has one of the top five lawyers in criminal law. She'll be here no later than ten a.m. The bitch won't let you speak with them one on one and neither will speak without her present."

What he hadn't said was this wasn't their first time arresting Young Castro and that the last time was a botched arrest. He wasn't the guy they were after at the time, but because of that, they'd caused him to retain a high-profile lawyer. One that wouldn't stand for any more botched investigations. Which was why the DEA hadn't brought him in. So, they had to think of something else.

Chapter Ten

A Memory

QUEENS, NEW YORK

"So, let me see if I got this right?" Young Castro said as he sat across from Unique inside White Castles.

For the past month now he'd been coming out to both Baisley projects and Forty projects to hang out with Unique. He'd even met a girl who lived in Forty named Asia. She was a Five Percenter too and had two kids. He'd been kicking it with her for 2 ½ weeks now, but he didn't know how serious the relationship was yet.

"This nigga Coogi that was getting high with my moms. The nigga owed Jameen some money?" he asked while looking across the table at Unique who nodded. "And the niggaz is saying Jameen gave them some bad dope?"

"That's what's been said, but I can't say for a fact how true it is," Unique said.

He watched as Young Castro took the time to process the information. Unique would have told him all this when they first met. Only he wasn't sure just how Young Castro viewed Jameen. Now he was pretty sure Young Castro knew that this nigga Prophet was the devil.

"Well, it's something to think about, "Young Castro said then went back to eating his fries.

The implications alone were enough for him to go back to Brooklyn and kill Jameen. If he was going to do that, he couldn't act off emotions. It had to be something he thought out carefully. Because he knew Jameen wouldn't die easily. Jameen he knew was a survivor. He'd witness the nigga come up out of some tight situations. In a couple of them, he was sure the nigga should have been closer to God.

"How come you ain't tell me none of this?" he asked.

"Well," Unique began explaining. "When I met you, it seemed like you and Jameen were thick as thieves. So, I didn't know how you would receive the information. Besides, all the junkies around your old apartment knew about it. I wasn't sure if you had heard the rumor or not."

Young Castro sat there and thought about it. He'd never even thought to talk with the junkies in his building. He was so sick of seeing his moms in that condition that he just kept a distance between himself and them.

"So, you heard it while you were dressing like a bum?" he asked.

Unique smiled. "You can learn a lot from a dummy," he said. "You'd be surprised at the stuff you could learn from that side of the streets. Most people avoid them. So, they never learn what junkies know," he further explained.

Young Castro considered that and the truth in the statement but what he really needed to do was find out what Jameen had going on with Coogi. To do that, he had to find Coogi.

$$$$

"What's on your mind, Papi? You look stressed out?" Asia asked.

Originally, she was Dominican, Puerto Rican, and Black, and just looking at her, an individual could tell. Asia was short, somewhere around 5'1 and beautiful, with long, black glossy hair and succulent lips. She wasn't superwoman thick, but she had a nice hourglass shape. So much so that you wouldn't have been able to tell she'd given birth twice.

Young Castro had been seated on the couch when she came in. Earlier, he'd stood outside and smoked a blunt and two cigarettes. Having respect for her cipher, she didn't want anyone smoking around her kids.

"Just some news I heard today," he stated as she took a seat next to him on the couch.

"Must be serious? You been quiet since I came home," she said.

Young Castro looked over at her. He knew that by quiet she meant he hadn't felt on her or tried to get some sex. Usually, whenever she was around him wearing those short-shorts like the dark blue ones she wore now. He kept a raging hard-on, but not tonight. Young Castro had thoughts of Prophet Jameen on his mind tonight.

"Nah, baby, it ain't nothing. Come here." He reached over and pulled her into his lap. They started kissing and he ran his hands all over her.

$$$$

"The fuck this nigga at when I need him?" Jameen was stressing. He pulled out his phone as he walked up the street. Then he put Young Castro's number in. The phone went straight to voice mail. He listened then said, "Yo' nigga, the fuck you at? I need some backup. This nigga Red Money acting funny about my shit. Yo' nigga, get at me ASAP."

He ended the call then looked around. Red Money was a Bloody G-Shine nigga that hustled out of Marcy. He owed Jameen $2600.^{00}. Money he should have been collected, but Jameen wasn't stupid. He knew he couldn't just run up into Marcy screamin' about getting at a nigga. Ever since the gang shit blew up. Niggaz been having a whole lot of body armor.

Nowadays niggaz fronted on niggaz because they knew they had fifty other niggaz standing around them. The coward in the middle really wasn't built like that but if you put fifteen soft niggaz together, you just might make one tough nigga. Individually they were bitches.

"This gang life done saved a whole lot of these fuck niggaz," Jameen said as he turned a corner.

He was so caught up in his thoughts that he didn't see the dark car creeping up behind him slowly. In fact, he wouldn't have been the wiser if he hadn't heard the doors when they opened. Jameen turned to look and that's when he saw the five figures with the red scarfs over the lower parts of their faces and he knew what it was.

$$$$

Young Castro exited the bathroom naked. He was tired and the shower he took relaxed him. On the bed, he saw Asia holding her phone to her ear talking to one of her friends. She was also naked. He had to do a whole lot just to keep his mind from focusing on her body. So, he reached for his pants and pulled his phone out. He saw that he had three missed calls and one voice message, which he listened to. Hearing Jameen stress about this nigga Red Money. He knew Red Money and he also knew that running up into Marcy wasn't an option. Either way, he needed to go see what was up.

"Listen, Ma, I need to go see what this nigga got going on back in Brooklyn," he told Asia. "But I'ma pull back up once this business is taken care of."

Young Castro got a text from Alexis while riding the train. But when he saw that it said Jameen was at the hospital he knew something crazy had happened. He called her.

"Hello."

"Yo' Ma, this Young what happened?" he asked.

That bitch ass nigga Red Money sent some of his boys over there to jump on Jameen. But he's a'ight, though. He'll be out tomorrow," she explained. "So, what's up? You coming through I've got a nice blunt."

And a wet pussy, he thought. "Yeah, I'll be there in about an hour. Have my stuff right when I get there, too."

"Alright, daddy."

When they ended that call, he sat back and thought about everything that was going on. He still didn't know how he viewed Jameen yet. One thing was for sure, though. He would find this nigga Coogi and see what the fuck was really going on. Then, if it was as bad as he thought it might be. Then he would have to figure out what to do about this nigga Prophet. Coogi wasn't the one who overdosed on some bad dope. His moms was and if it was because of the shit this nigga gave them. Then—

$$$$

Augusta, Ga

Present Day

The sun was beaming hard as both Young Castro and Jeeta stepped out of jail. Their lawyer was just behind them and they stopped.

"Okay, one question and don't either one of you bullshit me either." She looked into their faces. "Did you have anything to do with that undercover being killed?"

"Nah," Young Castro said. "Like I told them, we ain't kill nobody." He looked into her eyes. "We brought them guns from the person who might have done it. I'm not sure, though," he explained.

Diane Alexandria looked from him to Jeeta. She saw that he most likely would say the same. "Alright, well, here's the thing. Whoever this guy is, you two keep clear of him. You've got enough problems as it is. Those DEA guys have a file on you two," she said.

"Yeah, we sort of suspected as much," Young Castro said.

"Well, the file doesn't mean shit as long as you continue to be careful. The only thing about that is if they get enough on you, they could hit you two with RICO," she told them. "If they do. It'll be extremely hard to fight it. Which means neither of you needs to be seen doing anything criminal. Or caught with anyone who is," she said.

Young Castro thought about that. He knew some of what the RICO law covered. "What am I going to do about my business?" he asked.

She looked back towards the jail. "If you don't wanna end up doing Fed time," she began. "You'll find some other way to run your business. Because right now, I've got the feeling those guys back there are watching your business and the people who work for you. So, make some arrangements," she told them. She could see that they wanted to argue about it. "Listen the harder you make it for me to do my job. The more it'll cost you. So just move smart," she stated.

"Alright, we'll figure something out. Thanks for your help." They both shook her hand, then walked to the parking lot where Crystal waited in her Sky-blue Lexus LC 570.

$$$$

All three of the Blaylock girls were tall. Having received that gene from their father. Diane the oldest at thirty stood 5'10 and had a dark, honey brown skin tone. She weighed 146lbs and profiled it all in her measurements of 34-24-40. She was actually the shortest sister. Sabrina was the tallest, she stood right at 6'2 and at least 160lbs. All of which was athletically displayed because she kept in shape. She was, however, top-heavy, 36D-25, and 43 in the hips with only about 12% body fat.

Vanessa was the youngest; she was only twenty-three and known to be the most dangerous physically. Standing an even 6 feet and a good 150lbs she was the darkest and her slender frame was well-toned from earning her black belts. One in Kenpo which was a Japanese form of karate, expressing fewer kicks and more fluid movements with a lot of hand to hand combat. She also held a black belt in Wu'shu. A Chinese art form that she was good at. Her's was a mixture, it also combined Shaolin Quan which was Chinese boxing with empty hands. At the moment, all three sisters were seated inside California Dream.

"Girl where is your boyfriend? I have things to do," Diane asked.

"Me too, shit," Sabrina added.

Vanessa rolled her eyes and sucked her teeth. "First of all, he's not my boyfriend, "she said. "Not yet, anyway. I've still got this nigga Rook hanging around."

She would have explained further had she not looked up and saw Cream walking toward their table with another guy. This one stood about as tall as Sabrina.

"How you ladies doing?" Cream asked. "This is Ace, he's my right-hand. Do y'all mind if we sit?"

They all said no and waited while they pulled up chairs. Cream looked around the table, he already knew all of them. "What's up, D-Block—Brina?" he nodded.

Then looked over at Vanessa. Taking in the Gucci dress and Gucci heels she wore. Diane and Sabrina smiled as they caught the look.

"Ahem, I thought we were here to talk business?" D-Block interrupted his gazing.

"Yeah, my bad." Cream composed himself. "I imagine Nessa explained to you everything I spoke with her about?"

Diane smiled. "Yes, Nessa, told us that Young Castro wanted us to act softer."

"Well, not exactly softer," Cream explained. "One of the main reasons he likes doing business with you is that you're all tough. And you're beautiful." He watched them all smile at the compliment.

"Young doesn't want y'all to not handle your business. He just wants y'all to be more business-minded when you do it. He also wants me and Ace to be your back up," he said.

"More like babysitters." Sabrina laughed.

"Not really," Cream told her.

"Oh, you can continue doing your thing. He's cool with that as long as you're not bumping heads with none of our other people. But—" Cream paused.

"Come on with it. But what? "Diane asked.

"He wants y'all to be safe. In fact, he's already reached out to Damian, so D-Block is good, "Cream stated.

"Oh, really?" D-Block said. "I'll talk to Mr. Damian when I get home. Humm," she huffed.

Cream looked over at Sabrina. "He wants Ace to be your speed dial. Young says he really doesn't know these LOE niggaz like that. But with this extra product, you're about to receive. He'd rather our team be your back up," he explained. Then added. "And I'll be Vanessa's speed dial."

"I think we all knew that was coming." Sabrina laughed.

"Better watch out for that nigga Rook before you put your hand in that cookie jar, "D-Block said.

"Fuck you, D, "Vanessa stated. Then asked, "You mention an extra product?"

Cream looked around the table carefully. "Young is stepping up on your product, starting tonight. You're going to get fronted some extra weight," he said.

"Nigga quit playing," Diane said.

"How much extra?" Sabrina asked.

"You've been getting exactly ten keys, right? Well, you'll be getting twenty bricks from here on out. And with that much work you can see why he wants to make sure you're all safe," Cream said.

For a moment everyone was quiet. Processing the information. To the Blaylock girls, this meant a whole lot of money. It would also put a large target on their backs. From the cops and niggas who would want to try them.

"And we're getting the rest of that tonight?" Diane asked.

"Yeah, we've got it outside," Cream said. "I need Brina and Ace to exchange numbers."

They both pulled their phones out and did exactly that.

$$$$

Hernandez sat parked at the very back of the parking lot. He'd followed Sabrina to the restaurant. Trying to see if he could learn something more about these bitches. Then he saw the other two pull up and go inside. He'd been tempted to go inside himself until he saw the Cream-colored Range Rover Sport pull up. He knew who these guys were. Dawg had told him about them before he went missing. He still had a feeling that these guys had killed Dawg, but there was no proof. What did get him was that it seemed these crazy bitches were doing business with them. If that was the case, it would make things more complicated for him. He didn't know enough about these guys to be bumping heads with them yet.

Chapter Eleven

A Memory

Brooklyn, NY

"Ayo Sun I've got a bad feeling about this," Shakey said.

He glanced over to where Needles was pushing bullets into the old .38 that Prophet had given them to use on this job. The rest of the bullets, he slid into his pocket.

"Look, let's just hit the lil nigga and get it over wit'. We'll let Jameen worry about the extra shit," Needle said.

They both finish dressing and put their fitted caps on top of their heads pulled down. Needle would be the one with the gun. Him actually being the one Jameen gave it to. He still couldn't get over the fact that Jameen was this much of a slime ball, but everybody in the streets knew that Prophet didn't care about anybody but himself. He'd been like that for years. They were just surprised that this lil nigga hadn't figured it out.

$$$$

"Yo' let me tell you, nigga." Young Cas looked across the coffee table at the ugly nigga as he listened.

He was once again in Pink Houses at the apartment Jameen had sent him to a while back. Only this time he knew the Ugly nigga. Having gone back a number of times to buy packages. The niggaz name was Nasty. Or that's what he told Young Cas that they used to call him when he was a rapper. Young Cas thought that it had something to do with how the nigga looked. This nigga actually made Craig Mack look beautiful.

"You a bold ass nigga for sure duke." Nasty inhaled off the cigarette that hung from his mouth. He coughed. "The nigga Prophet ain't gon' be feeling you out here coping your own work."

"What he gon' do? Get mad because I wanna spend my paper on a package?" Young Cas asked.

"You see," Nasty started. "You see that right there is why I know you a green nigga. You talking like shit is some simple-minded shit. Like you can do what you really wanna do when you wanna do it."

Young Cas watched as he thumped the ashes off the tip. "Listen, duke, I don't get into niggaz business. But I can see you don't fully understand what you've gotten yo' self into wit' this nigga Prophet," Nasty stated.

Then, there was a long silence as it appeared Nasty was in the middle of some deep thoughts. "Jameen don't care 'bout nobody, Son. So, if you thinking you a special nigga, you stupid," Nasty warned. "The nigga will cut your throat probably faster than he'd cut mine. Wit' me, he wouldn't want to take the chance he'd miss. He knows I've got these guns up in here."

He waved at all the guns lying around. Young Cas looked at them. He'd come out to the Pink House to buy a package with the paper he saved. Jameen was home but still fucked up. So, he was laid up at his baby mother's trying to heal. Young Cas didn't remember how the conversation ended up being about Jameen in the first place. They were talking about something else at first.

For some reason, Jameen's name came up. "I know a whole lot of niggaz who wanna touch Jameen," Nasty said. "Prophet has enough enemies to share wit' a few niggaz. Only a fool would cross him, so don't be stupid, lil nigga." He put the cigarette to his lips and took a long hit.

Young Cas thought about it. His eyes took in all the guns that Nasty had lying around.

"Yo' you wanna sell one of these guns?"

"What you got?" Nasty asked.

Young Cas took a moment to think about it. He had nothing now. "I ain't got much. Shit, I just spent my last wit' you," he said, talking about the package he'd just brought.

He waited and watched as Nasty thought about it some more. Then he stood up and walked to another room. He came back a short time later holding a small .380. The gun didn't look like much, and it appeared to be old.

"This was the first burner a nigga gave me." Nasty stood there and looked down at the gun. "Reliable muthafucka, too. The bitch never jammed on me."

Young Cas watched him glance down at the gun that he held. It was almost like he had some fond memories he'd shared with the gun. Then Nasty looked up at him and shook the memories off.

"Look he started talking. "You an alright lil nigga. You still a little green and shit. But I fucks wit' you. And niggaz can't be out here hustling wit' out a piece. Especially when you fuckin wit' the devil—" He paused.

It was almost like he was about to make the toughest decision of his life. Especially concerning Prophet. A decision that was about to cost him too much. So, it deserved some serious thought. Young Cas watched as Nasty held the .380 out towards him. He reached out slowly and took the gun.

"So, what I owe you?" Young Cas asked.

Nasty shook his head. "You just be safe out there in them streets, young nigga. And come back to spend yo' paper wit' me," Nasty said. Young Cas looked down at the gun.

It wasn't like the .38 Jameen had let him hold. This .380 was smaller, but it didn't matter a bullet was a bullet.

$$$$

He left the train and walked the rest of the way on foot. At the moment, there were a lot of thoughts going through his head. The most vexing one being, how everyone seemed to know that Jameen was a black devil. Yet he continued to hang with the nigga. Those were his exact thoughts when he turned onto Church Avenue and saw Poe, Cream, and Dawg all standing out on the street corner hustling.

"Yo', what's the deal, Pah? You niggaz out here getting yo' paper right, huh?" he asked.

"No doubt, Son, no doubt." Poe laughed. "Niggaz is trying to get that trap house money like you getting nigga," Dawg added.

Young Cas really wanted to put them on, the truth of the matter was. He was still under Jameen himself. Technically, he was still a worker. He wasn't in no position to be putting other niggaz on. He was just starting to see his own fruits.

"Yeah, well time gon' come, Pah. And shit gon' change. We ain't always gon' be some low budget lil niggaz," Young Cas told them. Seeing as they were all around the same age. "But mark my words, bruh," he continued. "When that blessing do come. Yo', we gon' all enjoy it together. And we ain't gon' let the paper come between us, bruh," he stated, then continued. "When we get our shot, we gon' bless the game with the Rotten Apple people."

"Yeah, nigga, New York shit nigga," Pah added.

"Fo'real, New York shit," Cream threw his two cents.

They put everything on New York. Because New York was the heart of realness. The Rotten Apple was the Jungle that they were all bred within. To them, New York was home and their definition of Real Love.

$$$$

Young Cas entered his apartment and looked at all the trash lying around. He really needed to clean up. That or get him a permanent bitch. Seeing as he didn't want no bitch up under him that much. He started to clean up himself. Wanting to get that taken care of before he even started fucking with the dope.

Once he was satisfied with his cleaning. Young Cas went into the kitchen and removed a pot, a glass jar, and a box of Arm-N-Hammer baking soda. Next, he went back into the other room and got the cocaine, and the scale he was using to weigh everything.

"Now it's time to make the donuts," he said.

Young Cas sat about mixing and cooking the cocaine into crack. It really wasn't as hard as he thought it would be. He wasn't exactly a professional yet, but he was getting there. A few more packages and he'd be a made nigga. He took the pot off the hot plate and flipped the second slab of crack on to the table. He was just about to cook up another one when he heard the knock.

"The fuck?" he cursed.

Because he wasn't expecting anybody to come by and he wasn't into socializing, especially at his trap house. Shit like that was just stupid. Either way, he wiped his hands and went to answer the door. He left the .380 on the table, lying just under the corner of the newest source magazine he'd brought. Not thinking that he would need the gun. Even as he thought it while walking to the door. Something in the back of his mind kept telling him that he was being stupid. The knock at the door came again before he reached it to answer.

Impatient muthafuckas, he thought. "Yeah, yeah hold the fuck up," he called out.

Young Cas reached the door and removed the chain, then without thinking about it, he pulled the door open. The door was kicked hard as soon as it began to open. Catching Young Cas and sending him back to land on the living room floor.

When he looked up, he saw the two crackheads as they rushed into the room. One of them he knew he'd seen Jameen talking to before. He was the one with the gun. The other one closed the door and put the chain back on to it. He looked up with a serious unit on his face as Needle spoke.

"Listen, lil nigga," Needle said. "This shit ain't no personal shit. Niggaz just got a habit and not enough money to pay for it. And since you stupid enough to be trying to hustle solo. We just thought you wanted to donate to our cause." He smiled.

Young Cas watched as the other one seemed to lock in on the crack that was still on the kitchen table. Having just been cooked and not even cut yet. Young watched as he went over and grabbed a brown paper bag that the beer he'd bought at the corner store was in. The crackhead used the bag to collect all the dope Young Cas had cooked and the cocaine that hadn't been cooked. He even took the scale and box cutter. Once he had it all, he looked around to make sure he hadn't missed anything.

"You get everything?" Needle asked.

"Yeah, I got it all," the other crackhead said.

Needle looked back down at Young Cas as his partner walked back to the door. "Look ain't no need in you telling Prophet we hit you. Shit, the nigga respects grown man business. If I was you, I'd just take it as a learning experience," Needle said. He looked Young Cas straight in the eyes. "And get you some heat young nigga. In this business, everybody has some." Needle smiled and turned to leave. He paused just as his partner pulled the door open. "Oh, and if you still green when you get yo' next set up. Let a nigga know, we might want to come do some more business with you." He laughed at his own joke.

Young Cas sat there on the floor and watched as they turned and exited the apartment with all his dope. He took a moment to collect his thoughts. Then he stood up and grabbed the .380 off the table.

$$$$

"So, I'm like, yo just put the ashtray down. And we can talk about this shit," Poe explained.

The three of them, him, Cream, and Dawg were still standing out on the corner hustling. At the moment Poe was telling them about a fight he'd had with the girl he'd been seeing.

"And she like, nah, *fuck that shit nigga. I'm not going through this shit with you again,*" As he explained, Poe caught sight of the two crackheads as they exited the building. One of them carried a brown paper bag.

At first, he wasn't going to pay too much attention to them. That was until he saw Young Castro come out a few seconds later with a small gun in his hand. Young glanced both ways, then he turned in the direction the crackheads went.

"Yo' hold up, son. Let me see what this is about," Poe said.

Giving all his attention to the situation. As he turned to step off he pulled his 9mm out of his waistband. Both Cream and Dawg drew their guns too and followed. No one asked questions.

The Crackheads had turned up the next street. They caught up to Young Cas just as he reached the street. "Hey, Needle, you forgot something," Young Cas called out to them.

Both crackheads stopped, they were about halfway up the ally. Yet they turned anyway and stood there while Young Cas approached them.

"What young nigga? You still ain't learn yo' lesson? "Needle asked with a sneering look.

Young Cas stopped a few feet away. He was also aware of Poe, Cream, and Dawg having crossed the street to see what was going on. "Actually, I forgot to thank you for the lesson," Young Cas stated.

Then he brought his arm from behind his back and brought the .380 up. He watched as Needles' eyes grew in size. The other crackhead dropped the paper bag and turned. He set out running immediately.

"H—hold up, bruh," Needle began. "This was just some business shit. It wasn't personal."

Now it was Young Cas who smiled. "Yeah, nigga, and I just want you to know. I like the way you do business," he said in a deeper voice.

Young Cas squeeze the. The .380 wasn't loud, nor did it have a whole lot of kick to it, but it did get the job done. Poe, Cream, and Dawg watched as Young Cas unloaded the clip into the crackhead. Then his body dropped to the street.

"Yo' son want me to go get that other nigga?" Poe asked.

Young Cas looked up and he saw the other crackhead as he turned the corner at the end of the ally. "You think you can catch him?" he asked.

Poe shot past him before he finished speaking. The last visual he had of Poe was him holding a larger pistol in his left hand as he ran.

Young Cas moved forward and squatted down to pick up the bag with his dope in it. He then checked Needle's body and found the .38 that he'd drawn. For the second time, he remembered holding this same gun. That's when he realized that Jameen was the one who sent them at him. The devil actually made them do it this time.

$$$$

By the time Poe came back, they were all once more standing on the corner talking. Poe walked up breathing hard.

"Did you get him?" Young Cas asked.

"Yeah, the nigga tried to throw me off by trying to hide and shit, but I got him." Poe laughed. "But yo' what the fuck is up? Crackheads don't rob niggaz in Bedsty unless they really built like that," he explained.

For a second Young Cas was quiet, thinking. He owed Poe an explanation because he'd just killed someone because of him. That showed loyalty to him. "This nigga Jameen sent them," Young Cas said. He pulled the .38 out and looked at it. "I think the nigga was testing me. Trying to see if I could hold my own, but he just fucked up," He said and there was silence.

All three of them were looking at one another. Then Poe spoke, "Yo' listen, Son. We fucks wit' you the long way. Taking a few low budget niggaz out ain't shit. But going after the Prophet—" He paused. "Yo' son, that's a big order."

Young Cas wasn't surprised to hear that. Because even he knew that going after Jameen wouldn't be easy. "Nah, I'ma leave Brooklyn for a while," Young Cas said as he looked at them. "I got this Earth that lives out in Queens. I'ma go chill at her lab until I get my weight up. Then I'ma see about Prophet Jameen."

They all stood there listening. None of them believed that Young Castro would come out of that situation breathing. Not when they all knew Jameen's history.

"But listen, Pah," Young Cas continued. "Mark my words a nigga gon' come up. And when I do, I'ma come back for you niggaz. That's my word. Dirty Rotten Apple, nigga." He held his fist out.

"New York, nigga." Poe bumped his fist.

"NYC, nigga." Cream bumped his fist.

"New York City, nigga." Dawg bumped fist.

It was written in stone.

Chapter Twelve

Augusta, Ga

Present Day

"Young, you alright? "Jeeta asked as he drove.

He glanced over to where Young was sitting in the passenger seat. He seemed to be in deep thought because Jeeta had just been explaining some things to him and Young hadn't responded.

"Huh?" Young shook the memories off and looked over at where Jeeta drove. "What was that Pah?" he asked. Jeeta looked across at him carefully.

"You alright, bruh? You seem to be spaced out a lot lately. Something I need to know about?" he asked.

Young Castro broke eye contact and gazed out of his passenger's side window. He knew he would still have to go back to Brooklyn and do something about Jameen one day. He'd intended to do something before he left New York, but his grandmother's funeral came up. When he did go back to get Poe, Cream, and Dawg. Jameen had been on Rikers Island. Since then he'd heard from Asia and knew that Jameen was once more in the streets.

"Nah, Pah," he answered. "It's not something we need to worry about, right now. Let's just enjoy the club tonight."

They were headed to Francis Club, Caribbean Funk. Young Castro was actually going to meet up with Francis. They hadn't talked face to face in some time now and he'd been meaning to drop in. The thing with the Blaylock girls and then this thing with the cops. Everything kept causing him to put it off.

$$$$

113

Vanessa wasn't surprised by what she saw when she turned into Meadowbrook. She just thought that this nigga was smarter than that. Rook was originally from Meadowbrook and it was his main hustling area. About forty percent of the dope boys out there received their work from him. What they didn't know was, Rook received his work from her. She usually kept everything about business.

So, when she turned her Escalade into Meadowbrook and saw this nigga Rook standing in front of his old school, 65 Impala with that bitch Chelsea sitting on the hood. She wasn't jealous, that wasn't a word that she had intimate relations with, Nessa was disappointed. She even thought about not pulling up, but she'd had enough of this niggaz shit. So, she did pull her truck up, right next to Rook's ride. She saw his face change as he realized it was her.

The SUV was actually new, so he hadn't seen it yet. Vanessa looked into the back seat where five-year-old Toiya was watching cartoons on the LCD screen in the back of the headrest.

"Mama will be right back, you good?" she asked, Toiya nodded. Vanessa opened the door to get out.

Rook approached the driver's side fast. "Nessa, look, I can explain," he began.

She threw her left hand up and walked around him. She walked over to where Chelsea still sat on the hood of the Impala. Vanessa never had liked Chelsea, even when they were in school. Chelsea was one of those real light skin girls with green eyes and thought that she was all that. Even now, sitting there in her Dolce & Gabbana blouse, Perry Ellis jeans, and Gucci heels. She gave off the air of arrogance that Vanessa remembered from school. The bitch was beyond being stuck up.

"How you doing, Chelsea?" she asked.

"Oh, I'm fine, and you," Chelsea said sarcastically.

Vanessa smiled. "I'm good, I heard you had a boy. Did you name him after Rook?" she asked.

"I don't really think that's any of your business," Chelsea stated. "What me and Rook got going on ain't got nothing to do with you," she said.

Vanessa stood there and inside her mind, she could see herself doing a roundhouse kick. One that would send Chelsea across the hood of the Impala to the other side. But she wouldn't do that, it wasn't ladylike.

"You're right, well let me get on about my business." Vanessa turned and walked back to the driver's side of her truck. Not really acknowledging Rook's presence.

"Look just let me explain," Rook pleaded.

"Explain what?" Vanessa looked him up and down. "If it wasn't for the fact that Toiya needs her father. I'd dead yo ass right here in the street. But you ain't that important to my life—" She paused to glance back to where Chelsea watched them. "You and yo girl alright. And we gon' continue to do business together. But that's all we gon' do together."

She watched as the 6'2, brown-skinned nigga with the waves going to the side stood there looking stupid. Rook was a well-known nigga in the dope game. Both his pistol play and his fight game was serious.

"So, what does that supposed to mean?" he asked.

Vanessa pulled the door open and got into her truck. She let the window down and spoke out of it to him. "It means you only have two reasons to call me. And that is your daughter and my money. "She stated. "You'll still get the same prices on the work."

"But what if I wanna come by?" he asked.

"That ain't gon' be a good thing for you," Vanessa told him. Then added, "I've got this nigga I've been putting on hold thinking yo' ass gon' straighten up. But I can see that ain't gon' happen. So, you and Ms. Thang can do whatever y'all wanna do. I'ma do my own thang."

She started the truck and let the window back up. That was the end of her relationship with Rook. Vanessa pulled her phone out and text Cream as she drove off.

$$$$

"So, how's business been for you?" Francis asked.

The three of them were seated inside his office at the club. Francis was behind the desk, while they both sat in chairs in front of it.

"Business is alright, Pah. But we've got a lot of loot that we need to clean. So, I need your help big, bruh," Young said. Francis thought about it a moment.

"What about your detail shop?" he asked.

Young Castro shook his head. "Too much money, Pah. We already got the DEA and the ATF breathing down our necks. Niggaz try and push too much loot through that joint and we doing fed time for sure," Young Castro explained. "We need something more official."

"Do you have a business in mind? Something you'd want to get into that will bring in big money?" Francis asked.

Young Castro sat there a moment. "At first," he started. "I thought about doing this club thing like you got here."

"That would work," Francis said.

"But I'm also leaning toward opening my own car lot. Yo, a nigga already fucks with the cars. So, it won't be no odd shit to go down," Young Castro said.

"Yeah, but a regular used car lot won't bring in the kind of money you need. You can't even make it look like it is," Francis informed, slightly explaining the business to him. Then he paused in thought. He understood the problem, and he could almost see the solution.

"Listen, Rude, let me check with my people. I'm quite sure the old man will know a way to get it right. I'll get back with you in a few days," he said.

"A'ight, Pah, but tell him I got some other shit I need him to help me with, too."

"I'll just ask him if you can call him?" Francis said.

"No, doubt Pah, no doubt," Young Castro said.

Then he and Jeeta stood. "Now that I know you're on the job, big bruh. Me and my mans is gon' go out here and find some bitches to fuck."

Francis laughed, then thought about it seriously. "You do know that Raine still works here don't you?" he asked. Because that was a very important fact.

"Yeah, but she ain't gon' be back until my daughter Medina's old enough," Young Castro told him. "Don't worry, Pah. Niggaz ain't stupid."

Francis shook his head as they left the office. Then he pulled his phone out and sent a text to Big Dredd.

$$$$

"I can't believe this crazy ass girl," Ace spoke to himself as he walked through Krogers. "She needs this, she needs that. Shit, it's almost eleven o'clock. Why she ain't say shit earlier?" he continued conversating with himself.

He walked onto aisles where they had the items that Pam sent him to get.

He was busy trying to decide what to buy when the super thick, Hispanic woman spoke, "Frustrated, Papi?"

Ace looked at her, he didn't know the woman. But he did take a second look. Standing not five feet away from him, wearing a nice knitted full-length dress that seemed to embrace her body. The woman was *fine*!

"My girl getting on my nerves. Waiting till the last minute to ask for some shit," he explained and watched the woman stand there and smile.

"She must be a young woman?" she suggested.

Ace noticed that this woman had a little age on her. He'd guess that she was in her mid-thirties, but she could pass for a woman in her twenties.

"Yeah, how'd you guess?" He laughed.

"Young women spend the most time trying to confuse their men. It's sort of a game," she said.

"Speaking from experience, I guess?" Ace suggested and as he watched the woman smile, he couldn't do anything about the erection he was developing. "My name's, Ace." He held his hand out to her.

The woman shook his hand and introduced herself. "You can call me, Nita," she said.

"It's nice to meet you, Nita. I would stand around and talk more, but baby girl is waiting on this stuff," he said then as if he had an afterthought. "If you want, we can exchange numbers," he said, then watched that seductive smile stretch across her face.

"Sure, that is, if it's not going to get you into any trouble," Nita said.

"Nah, my girl doesn't go through my phone. And I don't go through hers," he told her.

They exchanged numbers and he turned to go pay for the items Pam wanted.

$$$$

Juanita watched as Ace walked away. As she stood there smiling, she also admired his build as he walked away. His swagger was nice, for a young man. She replaced the item she held in her hand. She hadn't really come into the store to buy it anyway. Her goal had been to meet this guy, Ace. The guy her brother pointed out some time ago while he was with the one called Cream.

Juanita knew all about Hernandez's so-called plans to take turf from these local drug dealers and she didn't agree with it, which was really the reason she'd moved her operations from Broad Street. She'd given Hernandez the excuse that she didn't think it was a good area to raise her ten-year-old son Hector. So, she moved to an area called Woodlake. She stopped at the freezers and opened them. She reached inside and grabbed a six-pack of Michelob Light. Then walked toward the counter. The truth of the matter was Juanita didn't think that her brother's plan would work. Hernandez was four years younger than her, and rather impulsive and sometimes tyrannical. Since he'd gained more power with the Mexicans, he'd brought to Augusta, he rarely listened to her advice.

She saw Ace as he exited the store and smiled. Placing the beer on the counter she lifted her Dior purse and removed the money to pay for it. Unlike her brother, she knew how to play the game. She knew that it wasn't always good to meet an enemy with force. Juanita could have nearly anything she wanted, not by force, but by seduction. Ace was about to experience in a very real way and she would continue her business, just not in the same method as Hernandez was going.

Chapter Thirteen

It was the first time that Cream had actually been to the Riverwalk during the day. Usually, it was one of those spots that you'd take a date after you ate and saw a movie. Today he'd decided to spend time with Vanessa and her daughter Toiya enjoying the quality time. He sat on one of the benches with Vanessa, eating ice-cream. While Toiya ate hers as she watched the speed boats race up and down the river.

"So, you and your baby father ain't rockin, huh?" he asked.

"Nah." Vanessa took a bite of her ice cream cone. Part of her hair fell across her left eye. She blew it out of the way as she looked up at him and smiled. "I caught that fool with his new piece. Told him it was a wrap," she stated.

Cream took a bite of his ice cream and thought over his next words. He didn't want to make any mistakes. "You do know I'm a New York nigga, right?"

"And what's that supposed to mean? I thought a nigga was a nigga. No matter where he was from," she stated.

"Not really." He polished his ice cream off. Then tossed the wrapper into the trash basket.

Cream sat in silence for a moment, searching for the right words to explain his reality. "If you were just a side piece or a quick nut. Yeah, then a nigga would be like every other nigga," he stated, looking into her eyes as he spoke. "But," Cream continued. "I've had this thing for you since I first met you. And it ain't about sex either."

Vanessa couldn't help smiling. "Oh, yeah, so what's it about then?" she asked.

"Truthfully," Cream said, then looked out to where Toiya stood, throwing rocks out toward the water. "A nigga tryin' to wife you. And have a couple of seeds wit' you. Shit—" He paused. "These streets take so much away from a nigga. I wanna see a family of my own before some nigga decides to put me to rest."

Vanessa turned and followed his eyes as he watched Toiya. Mentally she was going over what he said. She hadn't really thought about having any more kids. Toiya was five and in a couple more years she'd be going to school. Now that she'd heard him speak of more kids. She wondered how Toiya would feel about having a sister or brother.

"Being wifey is a serious job, you know?" she said.

"Yeah, I know." Cream smiled.

"And you're ready for some shit like that?" she asked.

He thought about it a moment. "Not really, but a nigga ain't getting no younger. Me and Poe the only ones who ain't got no seeds. I think his girl Nana is pregnant now. So shit, I want some, too," he explained.

Vanessa turned to look at him. "Having kids is bigger than just showing off to your boys. It takes a lot to raise them. Are you ready for that?"

Cream knew he would be a fool to rush into answering that. So, he took his time to think about it. "Yeah," Cream stated. "I think I can handle it."

$$$$

"Nah, nah, look, son," Poe stated as he walked up to where Tech 9 and another one of his workers were in the midst of an argument. They were arguing with a buyer that wanted some weight.

"Niggaz don't do break downs like that," Poe explained to him. "When niggaz go into their lab and cook up they shit. Heads is cooking what they intend to move. Ain't nobody working extra for no other nigga."

122

"Yeah, I understand that," the buyer said. "The only reason I asked for a setup is because Lil Tony and them over in Ginning's Holmes be droppin' the work. I just thought you niggaz were on the same page?"

Tech-9 watched as Poe looked at the buyer closely. Then he turned and looked at Tech. "Do I look like that nigga Lil Tony, son?" he asked Tech. Who shook his head. "Then please explain to me why this nigga giving me Lil Tony's M.O?" He looked around, but it seemed no one could answer. Then he looked at the buyer. Who in turn hunched his shoulders. "Listen, Son, I suggest you go on over there where Lil Tony doing his thang. And let Lil Tony break you off. Cause niggaz round here ain't on that shit," Poe stated.

Then they stood there and watched as the buyer's shoulders dropped. He turned and walked back to his ride. Once he'd left Poe laughed. "Son, da fuck wrong wit' these niggaz?" he said.

"I dunno, Thug," Tech responded. "I heard them niggaz over in Ginnings Holmes was on some competition shit. Trying to outdo niggaz."

"Yeah, but fuck," Poe said. "Sometimes it's not all about the quantity. Sometimes, son, it's about the quality of the material you're moving to. And I know our shit is good. Shit da God don't even put that much of a cut on the cook. Trust me, niggaz limping nowadays because of that same shit," he explained.

Tech already knew the history of his limp. That was a story he heard when he first started hanging with Poe. So, he knew how Poe felt he went out bad. Because he should have killed this nigga Pete Rose instead of beating him. So, Tech knew the lesson, the moral of the story. *'Dead niggaz don't come back at you.'*

$$$$

"Damn, I love the way you taste Ma. "Cream's words were a whisper in her ear.

Nessa shivered as he licked the lobe of her ear. In the background, Jaheim was preaching the word. Shivers ran through her from her ear all the way down to her sex and she became wet instantly. Vanessa glanced down and watched as his hands moved down across her bra. Having already removed her blouse. His fingers began to loosen the skirt she wore. Toiya was spending the night with her cousins at Vanessa's sister Sabrina's house. So, tonight was her night. She watched the skirt fall into a pool around her feet which was still wearing the Gucci stilettos she'd worn over to his place.

"We started out like Bobby and Whitney, Justin and Brittany. Then it all got ugly if it weren't for the money. They said I started acting funny, What's wrong with you honey?"

She gave a sigh of pure bliss as Cream laid her across his large bed and removed the rest of her things. Everything except the pumps.

"I love your shoes, Ma." Cream was kneeling on the bed on the side of her. His hands caressed her body slowly as he placed kisses on her neck and shoulder. "They make your legs look longer and sexy," he whispered.

Her lips parted as her breathing became heavier. Cream's hand moved down to caress and squeeze her breasts. She had two gold hoops piercing each nipple. When his fingers flicked the hoop she felt a jolt of pleasure that seemed to shoot straight down to her clitoris, that was also pierced, but with a diamond stud.

Cream pushed both of her hands up above her head as he moved down. He kissed each nipple and ran his tongue over the hoops. Drawing an intense response from her. She could feel her pussy as it moistened. She parted her thighs hoping that the cool air inside the room would lessen the intense sensations within her pink folds. That only seemed to make it worse.

Vanessa's eyes closed, but she was more than aware of his moving so that he was between her legs. Cream's hands ran across her thighs slowly, caressing each one as he raised them onto his shoulders. His teasing was driving her crazy. The throbbing within her pussy became so intense, she couldn't stop her hips from moving. Her back arched, pushing her pelvis with him.

Cream smiled, as he laid on his stomach between her legs. He bought both of his thumbs together at her center. He used them to part her folds. He blew his breath on her clit, just before his tongue reached out to taste her slit.

"Oh, shit," Vanessa chanted.

Seeing her reaction, Cream's tongue zeroed in on her clit. He even wrapped his lips around it and sucked. Then, as if things couldn't get any better for her. She felt him slip two of his fingers inside. Her pussy muscles began to grasp at the alien digits as they pushed into her velvety flesh slowly, then he found that spot.

"Oh, fuck," she moaned.

Her hips lifted more, pressing her pussy tighter to his mouth as Cream smiled.

"And I don't know how to get over her smile. I wonder what she's doing now? I think about her every once in a while."

She screamed as she came like a volcano erupting and he drank her every drop slowly. Vanessa reached down and held his head as he fed on her orgasm. Her body shook from yet another aftershock. Soon it became too intense for her, but she rode the wave out anyway. After several minutes she allowed her eyes to open. She saw Cream on his knees between her thighs. His face was wet with her juices, and she watched as he smiled.

She held eye contact as he reached down and grasp his dick. Then she felt him bring it into contact with the folds of her vagina, that was still wet and waiting. Vanessa felt him slide into her in one smooth, slow thrust.

"Oh, my God," she cried out.

While at the same time her body lifted toward his. Allowing him to fully penetrate her. Cream could feel her muscles as they tightened along the length of his dick. He felt her pussy moisten more, lubricating the way, making it easier for her to accept each of his thrusts. His dick seemed to go so deep until his tip somehow kissed the mouth of a womb before he withdrew slowly.

"I should have come with the ring. Set a date for next May. Guess I thought that you'd wait. Now I hate that I took so long, played around with her, now she's gone. Now my smiles turned to frowns, ups to downs. I don't know where I'm going now, I think about her every once in a while."

She couldn't sleep, Vanessa eased out of the bed without waking Cream. She was still naked but made her way to the bathroom where she turned the water on in the shower. Once she tested it to make sure the water was just right. She stepped under the spray. Vanessa thought about her life. All its goods and the bad. She thought about the things Cream said he wanted. It was only when she stepped into his house that she realized he didn't actually live like a thug.

Cream didn't live in Augusta. Instead, he had a nice two-story three-bedroom house across the bridge in North Augusta. The house was furnished like it was done by a woman. Truthfully it was actually better than her place.

Vanessa was trying to figure out just how serious he was about this relationship. Because she also wanted something real. She had a feeling that she could have that with him. Only time will tell, this she did know.

$$$$

Hernandez thought he had to give it to this guy Cream. Because he wouldn't have known that he moved the way he did, had he not been watching the bitch. He slowed the Cadillac CTS down as he approached the bridge. Having watched this guy's house long enough to know that the Blaylock girl would be staying the night. His reason for watching her was to see if she had any real weaknesses. He'd assumed that her daughter's father would be that weakness. That is until he realized she wasn't that much into him.

He's been following her since the day she found him with the light skin girl. He wasn't able to hear their words as they argued. He was however starting to believe that there was more truth to what Money Loc told him about these women. He was back in Augusta now and because this bitch Vanessa was involved with this guy Cream. He had to rethink his whole plan.

Hernandez didn't know for a fact what these guys had done with Dawg. He suspected that they killed him and got rid of the body. Yet, he wondered if Dawg told them that he was the one to tell Dawg about stealing their cocaine, that time he'd wanted to know how pure the coke they were using was. The only way to find that out was if he could sample it before they cooked it. So, he'd explained this to Dawg. Dawg said he was never present when the one called Young Castro cooked it. Nor was he with him when he went to get it.

In the end, he showed Dawg how to find out. Together they both watched the team from the shadows. As luck would have it, Dawg was the one to find out where they kept their cocaine. While he did bring back a sample of the coke so that Hernandez could test it. He'd gone missing before he could tell Hernandez where the cocaine was. Hernandez did know that it was too pure for them to have gotten it from another street dealer. He hadn't seen coke that pure since he'd left Mexico. So, he knew this Young Castro had to be connected and that was another problem.

$$$$

"Okay! So, what have we got?" ATF senior agent Sean Weston asked as he entered the office.

DEA Division Director Mark Hamon looked up from the papers he'd been going over. "I got a call from the lawyer. Diane Alexandria, she says her guys had nothing to do with the death of the undercover officer. She confirms that they received the guns from another party. Whom they only knew by the name of Baltimore.

Agent Weston took a seat and thought it over. "And you believe her?" he asked.

"There's no reason not to. Her clients don't even know that she was once with the District Attorney's office," Hamon said.

"Will she give us anything on these guys?"

"Never going to happen," Hamon told him. "She's not selling them out by giving us the name of this Baltimore guy. What she's doing is protecting her clients. At the same time pointing us in the right direction. Which also happens to be away from her clients."

Weston thought about it, while he appreciated the lawyer giving them some help. He still would like to get something on these guys. In his opinion, the criminals had more information than what they gave her.

"Okay." He let out a deep sigh. "I'll have my people look into this Baltimore character. See what we can find," he said.

He still wasn't going to forget about these two guys. He had a feeling that they would all cross paths again.

Chapter Fourteen

It was real late by the time Juggernot stepped outside of Club 360. After 3:00 a.m, he knew it was closer to 4, but he made it to his ride without stumbling and falling on the way. The Chrysler 300 SRT was new, he'd only had it for a week. Even the inside of it still smelled new. Using the button on his key chain he disarmed the alarm, then unlocked the door. He was just in the process of pulling the door open when a dark blue BMW 2 Series Coupe pulled into the parking lot two cars over.

His head came up, not because he knew the car, but because of the woman he saw getting out. Juggernaut watched as the thick Hispanic woman exited the car. She paused as she closed the door. Then, not looking around she opened her purse and dug inside. He watched as she removed a pack of cigarettes and took one out. Then she looked for a lighter, which it seemed she couldn't find.

"You need a light?" he spoke up.

The woman turned to acknowledge his presence. "If you don't mind," she said.

Juggernaut left the door open as he turned and walked toward her. He dug into his pocket and pulled out his own lighter. He held it up and cupped his other hand around so that the wind wouldn't blow the flame out. Then he struck it for her. He looked in her face and smiled as she bent forward to light her cigarette.

"Thank you," the woman said as she puffed a few times. "You made this too easy for me."

Juggernaut gave her a confused look. Then he noticed that her hand had still been inside the purse. He watched as she withdrew it and saw the Beretta 9mm with the silencer attached to the end of it. Juggernaut was confused. He looked up into the woman's face.

"What?" he tried to speak.

She pointed and squeezed the trigger. Juggernaut's body did a slight dance as he took a couple of steps back. The woman continued shooting, placing a total of eight shots into him. She watched as his body fell and landed at the back of another car. He shook for a moment and while he did this she glanced around to make sure that no one was paying attention.

Juanita then replaced her gun and pulled out a blue handkerchief which she tossed onto the body. "Somebody had to be the sacrifice," she spoke. Then she returned to the BMW that she needed to get rid of. The whole point was her brother was taking too long to start his little war and this guy Juggernaut was in control of one of the largest turfs. The entire Sunset area. From Lucky Street back to the train tracks. He ran it all by himself, she had plans for that area.

Juanita was wondering why her brother hadn't gone after this guy in the first place. Instead, he wanted to stalk these women, which was stupid. She backed the car out and left the parking lot. This would start something, but it would also make her brother focus on his real issues. While she focused on her own plans.

The news about Juggernaut reached Jeeta first. Mostly because of the blue handkerchief. When word hit the streets, it was assumed that the Crips were the ones that killed him. When Jeeta questioned his people, they were all present and accounted for and their alibis were solid. Which was why he picked up Young Castro.

"So, we gon' dead these niggaz?" Young asked. Riding in the passenger seat of the Escalade ESV that Jeeta drove these days.

"Not exactly," Jeeta said. "Remember, we've got that trip to Atlanta coming up. We have to buy those cars and set up this car lot. Washing our money is at the top of the list."

"Yeah, yeah, Pah." Young lit up a cigarette. "Because this is still business. But disrespect don't go unchecked either."

They rode in silence, both of them thinking and trying to put the pieces together.

"Besides, I'm not so sure these niggaz did it," Jeeta said.

He made a turn, and they were soon pulling into Harrisburg. It didn't take long before they came into the area where Money-Loc controlled. Jeeta found a place to park.

"Yo' I'm keeping my burner on me," Young said as he pushed the FN Five-Seven into his waistband.

Jeeta checked his SP-Taurus. "Wouldn't have it any other way." He smiled.

They exited the truck. The whole neighborhood was crawling with Crips and Mexicans. Jeeta would have brought some of his homies or Young could have brought Poe, Cream, Tech, and Ace, but that would speak volumes.

"Listen, bruh," Jeeta said. "I know your status. But you gave me the job of running the streets. So, this has to play out the right way. Don't let this nigga make you mad. Because I'm still not sure these niggaz did it yet," he explained.

"Look, Duke, you do your thang." Young smiled. "Just think of me as your backup."

Having that understood Jeeta turned and Young followed as they walked up to Money-Loc's main trap house. When they reached it, they found Money-Loc and a few of his homies standing around working on a 63 Impala. Money-Loc looked up when they turned the corner.

"That boy, Jeeta. I been expecting you, cuz." He smiled.

Jeeta continued to look at his crew. Because the smile itself wasn't exactly a friendly smile. "So, the cops questioned you about the murder, too?" he asked.

"Not me directly. They pulled Tru-Loc and Lil' Snoop in and asked them some questions," Money-Loc explained.

Jetta looks over to where Tru-Loc and Lil Snoop stood on the other side of the Impala. "They must have had an alibi then?" he said.

"Tru-Loc was at work, and Lil Snoop was at his grandmother's that night. Lots of people saw him there," Money-Loc explained. "Me, Jay-Loc, and C-Loc were all inside club Cloud 9 until about 5:30 that morning. Wasn't no need to question us too much." He smiled, then asked. "What about your homies. They all in the good?" he asked.

"Yeah, they good." Jeeta watched as his eyes moved to land on Young Castro.

"What about him?" he asked.

"Yo', Pah, all my people were good," Young said defensively.

Jeeta jumped in and put a stop to that. "Listen," he began. "I'm just trying to find out who did it and want to make it look like some Crips did it. That's all! If it wasn't your homies. Then somebody wants us to think that it was," Jeeta outlined.

Jeeta and Young Castro watched as Money-Loc's face took on a look of concentration.

"What?" Jeeta asked. "You know who might have done something like this?"

"I'm not sure really," Money -Loc responded.

They waited but it didn't seem like Money -Loc was going to tell them who he suspected. Jeeta looked at Young Castro. Then he looked back at Money-Loc.

"Listen, whoever did it. They don't care about you and your homies. If shit goes down, them fools gon' be the one's sitting on the sideline. Waiting for the smoke to clear," Jeeta told him.

"So, what you saying, cuz? Me and my homies won't be the last ones standing?" Money-Loc asked. His eyes looked Jeeta up and then down. Next, he sized up Young Castro, who he watched as Young hunched his shoulders. "Besides," Money -Loc continued. "Crips ain't the only ones with blue flags. I thought you knew that Homie."

When he said it, a certain reality dawned on Jeeta. The so-called conflict that Money-Loc hinted at before. The one between the Crips and the Mexicans. MS-13 flagged the color blue, too.

Jeeta threw his hands up. "Hey, we good cuz," he said. Then looked at Young Castro. "Come on, let's get outta here."

Money-Loc stood there and watched as the two of them walked away. He really didn't have any love for either one of them. Even less for the New York nigga. At the moment, what he didn't appreciate was this Spic muthafuckas trying to set them up.

$$$$

"Yo', what's on yo mind, Pah? How you feelin'?" Young asked.

They were back in the truck. Jeeta sat there deep in thought. He hadn't even reached to start the truck. "You know them Mexican muthafuckaz that nigga Dawg was talkin' about?" he asked.

"Yeah, fuckin' Hernandez. What about him? That nigga been quiet lately," Young Castro said.

"Too quiet actually," Jeeta told him. "Mara Salvatrucha is an EL-Salvadorian gang. They call it MS-13 out West. And they flag white and blue. A lot of the time people mistake them for Crips. Some of that is because there's usually no beef between them and the Crips."

"And you think this muthafucka is MS-13?" Young asked.

"Look around lately, bruh. You been seeing all these Mexicans moving in." Jeeta pointed out. "Usually, when Mexicans move into a neighborhood. They'd get one or two houses. And start moving more families in. At first, everybody would be living under the same roof. They would be saving their money up and growing larger. Once they've got enough, they'll buy another house, then another. Before you know it, they have a community."

"Like up on Central Avenue?" Young pointed out.

"But I don't think Central Ave is big enough for what they got going on these days," Jeeta said. Then paused in thought for a moment. "What you think about us taking a ride over to Central Ave?" he asked.

"Son, I'm sitting in yo' passenger seat. Ain't you the one driving?" Young stated.

Jeeta started the truck.

$$$$

The fact that he shared the majority of his trap area with Juggernaut, kind of made it hard for Ace to move as much weight. When word came that Juggernaut had been killed, most of the buyers who'd been getting weight from him were pulling up on Ace.

He sat on the bleachers behind the Rec-Center and watched as the two buyers returned to their rides. The way Ace had it set up was, he didn't actually make any transactions. What he would do is sit out on the bleachers. When someone came to make a large buy. They would park their car close to the recreation center, walk to the bleachers, and take a seat. Usually, there were some guys out playing basketball. So, it would look like they were watching the game. In truth, what was really happening was the package would be placed into their rides while they sat there. The money was dropped off when they stopped at the store at the end of 15ᵗʰ street.

Once the money was picked up, a text would be sent to Ace's phone telling him in code how much money. Ace would in turn text another party that was in a house over in Dunn's Lane. They would bring the desired package to the center. While the buyer sat there talking with Ace about the game. The package would be placed in their ride. Ace would receive another text, then he would text the amount of the product to the buyer's phone. To the average person, it would seem complicated and may be stupid to some degree.

However, by doing the deal this way separating the money from the actual drug. It would make it nearly impossible for the DEA to say the buyer purchased the drugs. If the cops happen to pull the car over leaving the center and find the package the buyer could safely claim someone else placed the package into their ride. There would be no fingerprints and no financial transaction to prove something was sold, and something was bought. The buyer would lose the money but because of Ace's system. Ace would give them the same package at half price. If they could factually prove the cops took the first one.

By doing his deals this way, Ace never touched anything in the open, money, or product. So, that the DEA couldn't factually say that he sold anybody anything. The whole system was designed by some guy in the Feds that Young Castro knew. Young met him through this guy Francis. Big Dredd was an old drug kingpin that was doing fed time.

Ace didn't know much about that whole situation. Just enough to trust that the method worked. From what Young told him. Big Dredd beat all his sales cases this way. The Federal Prosecutor convicted him on other charges, none of them were sales cases.

Ace watched as the two rides exited the parking lot. Now that Juggernaut was out of the picture he would be making way more money. The thing about that was, now he wondered if he had to watch his back. Just as he thought that his phone rang. Ace looked at it and saw that it was an unknown number.

So, he answered, "Yeah?"

"Are you busy?" the female voice asked.

Ace screwed his face up because he didn't recognize the woman's voice. "I'm at work, right now, but I can talk. Who is this?" he asked.

She laughed seductively. "This is Anita. Remember, from the store the other night?" She told him.

Bringing the image back to his mind. "Oh, yeah, yeah. How you doing, beautiful?" Ace asked, then said, "No disrespect, but that was like a couple of weeks ago. And since I hadn't heard from you. I didn't know what was up on your end."

"Well, you had my number, too. You could have called," she told him. "But I've been working myself. I just happened to have a little time, so I called."

"Oh, so you're at work too, huh?" he asked.

Juanita sat inside of the smoke grey Dodge Charger SRT Sedan. Parked further up the street from the Rec-Center. The car had dark tint windows, so anyone walking by wouldn't have been able to look inside and see someone unless they came in close. "Yeah, I guess you could say that," she said. "I'm sort of on my break, right now."

She watches as Ace leaned back on the bleachers to get comfortable. She could see the smile on his face. "I would have called, right, but I didn't want to look like I was stalking you or some shit." He laughed.

Juanita laughed, too. *If only you knew,* she thought.

She didn't see Ace as a threat, he was more like a project to her. Especially if the plans she had worked. The direction she chose to take was one totally different from her brothers. Killing Juggernaut was a necessary killing. Because she needed this guy Young Castro to be focused.

"You think that your girl would mind if you and I met?" she asked, she really didn't care if his girl did mind.

"What you mean, like later?" Ace asked. He thought about it a moment. "How about we hook up around." She watched as he checked the time on his watch. "I get off in a couple of hours. I could meet you at the mall around six. And we can get something to eat. That is, if you're off work by then," he explained.

Juanita smiled, knowing her time was her own. "Yeah, I get off in a couple of hours, too," she told him. Mentally she was thinking, her plan might just work.

Chapter Fifteen

"You about ready to let me deal with the situation, Pah?" Young Castro asked looking across the table at Jeeta.

They were sitting inside Captain D's, having already eaten. It was now a full month after Juggernaut had been murdered. The police had no leads and while Young Castro sat back, allowing Jeeta to handle his business. There hadn't been anything done as of yet. When they went to Central Ave. They hadn't seen Hernandez but Jeeta was able to show him the many Mexicans that walked around rocking the blue bandanas. Young Castro watched as Jeeta sat there deep in thought. He knew that it was a matter of pride. Jeeta didn't want to admit that this might be too large of a problem for him.

"Man." Jeeta sighed. He looked up into the other man's eyes with frustration in his own. "This shit is crazy. I know what I suspect. I even know what I wanna do about it." He fell silent. Falling deep into his thoughts.

"But?" Young Castro asked. "Yo' Pah, I hear a but in there somewhere."

"Listen, Young, I just don't want to make the wrong decision. What if it ain't this spic muthafucka? What if it's these niggaz Money-Loc and his team playing some type of chess game and shit?" Jeeta speculated, his eyes still on Young Castro. Who leaned back into the seat he sat in casually.

Young Castro looked around them at the other customers enjoying their food. Not one of them looked like they had a problem. A lot of them were wearing suits, so he guessed they were businessmen.

"You know, son," Young Castro began. "I can remember when just the thought of sitting up in an establishment like this, eating good was only a dream—" He paused and watched a kid walk by outside talking on his phone.

"There was a time when I dreamed about rocking jewels and fly clothes. But every day when I woke up, I would be forced to deal with my reality." Young Castro turned and looked across the table at him.

"My reality, Pah. A nigga went to sleep hungry many nights. There were even nights when a nigga couldn't sleep because the hunger pains were just too noticeable," he said.

Young Castro sat there and looked into Jeeta's eyes. Allowing him the time to think about what he said, "Son," he continued. "Life is filled with fucked up decisions. And we all have choices in life. Me—I chose to run with a snake ass nigga who was my ticket out of a situation. I didn't like the decision I made. In fact, I grew to hate it in time. But do you know what the truth of it all was?" he asked.

Jeeta shook his head. "I learned to accept my reality. And live with my choices. Be they right or wrong. I always did what I thought was the right thing to do for Young Castro," he finished.

They sat there in silence some more. Jeeta was thinking about how he never had to live the life that Young Castro had lived and he tried to understand it. Jeeta just couldn't visualize himself homeless the way Young said he was after his moms died.

"So, what would you do in this situation?" he asked.

Jeeta watched as Young Castro dug into his pocket and pulled a roll of money out. He peeled off two twenties and placed them on the table. Then moved to slide out of the booth. "Come on, son, we still gotta go see Francis," he said.

They both got up to leave, Jeeta didn't speak again until they'd stepped outside and were almost to the Denali. "You asked if I was about ready to let you handle the situation. But you didn't answer my question," he said.

Young Castro stopped once they reached the truck. "You putting too much thought into it, Pah. We both know this nigga Hernandez got to Dawg. So, we know he's a threat. Which means eventually we gon' have to dead his ass anyway. And them niggaz Money-Loc and his team." Young Castro looked straight into Jeeta's eyes. "Son, even I can see you gon' have to kill that nigga. The nigga don't mean you no good. So, it doesn't matter which one did it and is trying to set the other one up. We just dead both them muthafuckaz and be done with the whole thing," he explained.

Young went ahead and walked to the passenger side door. He'd said what he had been thinking since Juggernaut had been killed. To him, it really didn't matter who got it first. Because his mind was already made up. They were both going to get it anyway.

$$$$

Vanessa sat up on the hood of her SL-Class convertible that was the 2011 edition, silver, and grey. The Mercedes-Benz was parked in her driveway. She was wearing Donna Karen shorts and a Parasuco blouse and Jimmy Choo platforms. While Cream stood between her legs as they both watched Toiya playing in the yard with both of Sabrina's kids.

That was the scene when the dark blue Lincoln Navigator pulled up to the curb. When she looked back and saw Rook exit the truck, Vanessa thought Cream would move. But he didn't, instead, he stood his ground. So, when Rook walked up, she was already prepared for the bullshit.

Cream didn't feel any type of way about the nigga. Not when she'd made it a point that they were together now. So, when Rook stopped in front of them, Cream looked the nigga up and down. They were both about the same height, 6'1 give or take a few. But Rook weighed more than him by about 10lbs and was slightly more muscularly built.

"What's up, my nigga? "Rook said It was almost as if he had to force the words out of his mouth,

"Sup, Son?" Cream replied.

"You, uh—mind if I have a word with Vanessa?" he asked.

The way Cream was standing, Vanessa was behind him. She had her arm wrapped around him with her chin on his shoulder.

"We can talk about business in front of my man," Vanessa told him. Cream watched as the niggaz face twitched.

"Look. Rook started. "I'm trying to be respectful about this. I just need to speak with you in private for a minute."

Cream couldn't see her face, but he was pretty sure that she was smiling right now. All women were vindictive.

"Boy, I know you ain't in your feelings, right now?" She stated, being funny. "Didn't I tell you that ain't nothing personal between us anymore? If you got something to say about the work I'm bringing to you tomorrow. Nigga you can say that shit in front of my man."

Both she and Cream watched as Rook looked Cream up and down. Sizing him up more than likely. "I don't know why you tripping. It ain't even gotta be like this," Rook said.

"Trippin?" Vanessa said "Nigga, if me and Cream were together and his ex- asked to talk to him in private. I'd think he was still fuckin' the bitch. So, do you think I want my nigga to think me and you still fuckin." she asked and watch as the stupid look came over his face. Rook parted his lips to speak but couldn't. "Exactly," Vanessa said. "Ain't no secrets between me and my nigga. So, if you got something to say

then say it. Cream remained silent. He wasn't about to get into her business. He did appreciate the way she handled the situation. Because he probably would have done the same thing.

$$$$

Rook was pissed as he drove away. He couldn't believe this bitch had handled him like that in front of this nigga. Granted, what he had to talk to her about wasn't what he said. He had to make something else up. Because he hadn't expected her to have a nigga over there when he decided to pull up.

He and Chelsea were having problems. So, he thought that he'd just pull up and see if he could fuck something with his baby's mama. When he pulled up and saw the nigga. It was too late for him to turn around. So, he had to make some shit up. Still and yet, he didn't appreciate how the bitch just played her little game, but he had something for her punk ass, though.

$$$$

"You gon' have problems outta that nigga one day," Cream told her as he watched the truck pull off.

"Pissh." Vanessa rolled her neck. "That bitch ass nigga ain't crazy. He knows I will fuck his life up. If he even thinks about acting stupid out loud."

Cream couldn't help but laugh. "Yeah, I know you all gangster and shit. But no nigga likes to be chomped off publicly. Trust me, that nigga ain't happy about the way you handled him," he explained.

There wasn't anything else that he could say after that Rook was her problem. He was just hoping the nigga didn't get too far into his feelings about this situation. Because if he decided to run up on him about it. Things weren't going to end good for him.

$$$$

Poe pulled the Range up to the car detail shop that Young Castro ran. The Detail shop sat on Deans Bridge Road and was known to do everything from painting to bodywork, and hydraulics and rims. It even installed stereo systems if the customer wanted that done. When he stepped out of the truck, his partner Tech .9 exited the passenger seat. Together they walked to the Detail shop. One of Young Castro's workers looked up as he saw them approaching.

"Yo', son, is my mans in his office?" Poe asked.

The worker nodded, then went back to taping off a Ford Mustang that they were about to paint.

Poe put that to the side as he continued to lead the way to the office. Once there he tapped on the door.

"Yoo'?" Young Castro called out.

Poe opened the door and they stepped inside. Young Castro sat behind his small desk. While Jeeta sat over on the couch. At the moment, Young was on the computer and Jeeta was texting on his phone.

"Da fuck is up, son? You sounded like y'all was about to go kill niggaz when you called." Poe looked from Jeeta over to where Young looked from his computer with a smile on his face. *That's disturbing,* he thought. "Slow down, Pah. The killing ain't gon' happen, right now. But it's gon' happen, "Young Castro stated.

He watched as Poe looked around the office as if he was lost or something. Maybe even confused a little. "Yo', is it safe to talk in this muthafucka? Or should I be speaking the language?" he asked.

The language was the Five Percenter dialect. Which in New York nearly everybody knew even if they weren't Five Percenter. They'd hear it so much that to them it became a common speech.

"Nah, you good, Pah. I sweep the muthafucka myself whenever I come in," Young Castro said.

"Yeah, cause nigga you got me thinking about, Racketeering Influenced and Corrupt Organizations Acts. Muthafuckin' RICO shit can take anybody down and shit," Poe said.

"Yeah, well, we good right now. But yo son, I need you to do something for me," Young Castro stated. "I've got this shipment of cars coming at the end of the week. We gon' start-up this exotic car lot soon. So, I'ma need you to buy the shop from me," he explained.

"You wanna sell me your shop?" Poe asked.

"Yeah, it's going to take me and Jeeta to run the car lot. And since these are some expensive cars. Neither one of us will have the time to run this place," he explained.

Through Francis's connection, Big Dredd, he had been able to visit Georgia's Government Siege Auction. An auction where the Government sold off all the properties they'd confiscated during drug raids. Until Big Dredd had two tickets sent to him, he had never heard of it. Nor had he expected to see the types of rides that were being sold for cheap. Aston Martins, Audi's, Bentley's Jaguars, Lamborghini's, and Ferrari's.

Young had heard that the Government resold these rides that they took from drug kingpins. But he never knew how they did it until a couple of weeks ago. "Son, why you wanna sell the muthafucka to me. Did you ask Cream if he wanted it?" Poe asked.

Not that he didn't want it. The Detail shop did a lot of good business and brought in some serious money.

"Nah, Pah, I kinda got something else that I want Cream to get into. But the thing is, with these muthafuckin' DEA niggaz watchin. Headz is gon' have to have some ways to make their money, good money," Young Castro explained. "Big Bruh's people gon' help us navigate our way through the bullshit. And to do that, all my top niggaz gon' have to be doing their own thang."

When he spoke to Big Dredd about it. The older man had explained that they would need at least three different businesses and that those businesses needed to be separated. Not working as one business with many levels. The way Big Dredd explained it if each business could be linked together in any type of financial way. Then the Rico law could still be used.

"Okay, so how much you want for it?" Poe asked.

"A hunnid grand."

Poe let out a long whistle.

"But that's why I asked you to bring your mans with you," Young said. "That's the number that'll go on to the sale's papers. But that's not what you'll pay. Together both of you just give me $8,000.^{00} apiece."

Poe looked over at Tech.9 who looked at him. They were both thinking serious about all this. "What's up, you in son?" Poe asked.

"Yeah, I can come up with eight grand," Tech 9 stated.

Then Poe looked back at Young and smiled.

Young Castro looked back at his computer as Poe and Tech 9 left. He'd been studying The Franchise 500 by Industry. Getting a feel of how to establish a business with a reasonable amount of funds. Big Dredd had already had one of his banks front him a loan to buy the cars and the building he would sell them out of. But he said that someone on his team should open one of these small Franchise Businesses. Not something like McDonald's or Sonic. Those were actually too big for a local street hustler to jump into. At first anyway, maybe a later project though.

However, the startup cost for a Baskin-Robins was between $93.6k to $401.8k. Which was within reason of the loan Big Dredd said that he could have another bank give Cream.

It really wasn't a loan actually. In truth, Cream would have to give a certain amount of money in cash to Big Dredd's people. The bank would grant him a loan for that amount. Young Castro already knew that Cream had a little over $175,000.00 put away. So, he was going to add $25,000 to that and have him get a $200K loan to open the Franchise. But he still needed Cream to clean his act up and put on a business front. Since he was the only one of them to graduate and had at least sixteen months of community college under his belt. Cream was the best one for this business. All eyes would definitely be on his team when they made these types of moves. Cream was the best one for this particular move.

Chapter Sixteen

"We argued like Archi and Edith. Like Ike turned on Tina. But I really didn't mean it, I was raised not to hit a woman, never raise my hand – especially not the one I'm lovin,"

Jaheim

Diamond In Da Ruff

"Yeah, I got something for this bitch," Rook mumbled as he took in the smoke from the weed.

He was actually smoking what was called a *dirty*, where the weed was mixed with something else. His was mixed with the twenty-dollar piece of crack that he'd crushed up earlier. Rook sat inside his Navigator and hit the blunt once more. As he held the smoke deep inside his lungs, his eyes glanced around at the scenes outside of the truck. He was sitting there parked at a gas station not far from Meadow Brook.

As a rule, he never smoked like this around his crew. He didn't want to give off the wrong impression. Right now, he wasn't thinking about his crew. His mind was focused on this bitch Vanessa and how she tried to play him. Pride wasn't about to let him go out like a punk, which was why he was getting ready to see about this nigga she was calling her new nigga. Rook already knew where to find the nigga.

He found out that this fool has something going on over in Governor's Place. Rook looked over at the passenger seat, lying on it was the 9mm he was able to use and the ski mask he would be wearing. To him, the logic had been, pull up, flex like he came to see his daughter. Then start a conversation with her. One where he would put his game down and slide his way back between her nice sexy thighs. He hadn't really believed her when she said she had a nigga on standby to take his place. After all, they'd been through? Nah, he didn't really believe that until he pulled up and saw it with his own eyes.

Rook was a playa, he'd always been a playa. In middle school, high school, on the streets. That was his M.O. So, he could recognize another playa when he saw one. This New York nigga didn't strike him as a playa. He couldn't see no any type of nigga pulling a bitch from him. That shit just didn't make any logical sense.

He never took it seriously that shit was over between them. It wasn't like Vanessa had just found out about Chelsea, and that she was pregnant by him. That shit was old news and they stayed together. He'd been able to talk his way through it, hit her off with some good dick and it was over. That's how shit usually went between them until now that is.

"Yeah, I'ma show this bitch," he mumbled.

Rook just couldn't believe that Vanessa had tried him like that and the bitch knew his M.O. "It's a'ight this nigga about to feel it, though," he preached to himself and the gun while smoking.

$$$$

"So, how's that business coming?" Cream asked as he walked around the pool table.

He was looking for a good shot. Not really liking the way that the balls were set up on the table. Ace, on the other hand, stood there holding his cue stick.

"I've got everything in order," Ace began. "I'm already in the process of putting my nigga Shine in position. Let him handle the work while I rock wit' you."

Since Young Castro wanted Cream to open a Franchise business because he'd taken college classes for business. Cream had asked that Ace go into it with him, which meant that Ace wouldn't be able to hustle the streets directly. Neither one of them could have their name coming up in any criminal activities while indulging in this type of business.

"Just look at it from the good side," Cream stated as he leaned across the table and prepared to take his shot. "We'll be able to clean our bread before we make these sandwiches. Especially since Young got us making a whole lot of sandwiches these days."

Ace laughed. "Yeah, I know right," Ace had to admit.

Since he'd joined the team, he was making damn near four times what he'd been making on his own. However, some of that was also because Juggernaut had been killed. His death left a serious void in the area and thankfully, Cream was able to get him a larger shipment.

The little nigga Shine had actually been on his team since before he met Young Castro. He'd been a top of the game hustler. He just hadn't had the type of access that Ace was giving him now.

"Truthfully," Cream said. He stood across the table and watched as Ace took shots. "I've been thinking about getting on some serious good boy shit anyway."

"What?" Ace laughed and looked at him disbelievingly.

"Nah, Son, serious shit," Cream added. "Since me and ma done got on this relationship vibe. A nigga been thinking about family shit."

They were both quiet after he said that. Both thinking over the words and their implication. "You know what, bruh?" Ace stood up straight and looked directly into Cream's eyes. "Nigga, I really do feel that shit."

Cream smiled, what he didn't tell Ace was that for a moment he thought that maybe he was getting soft. That he was allowing what happened to Poe, and then Dawg to get to him. He feared that he wasn't as street as he'd been when they left New York. So, Ace's words meant a lot to him because he understood the move. More than what Ace may have realized

$$$$

They both stepped outside of the pool hall, laughing at a joke as they walked toward the Yukon Denali that Ace was driving these days. The truck itself was still painted a factory green. Only because Ace hadn't had the time to get it painted yet. As they reached the SUV, Ace walked around to the driver's side, while extracting his keys from his pocket. Cream walked around to the passenger door.

As he reached forward to grasp the door handle, Cream caught sight of a reflection in the window. He saw a figure approaching, behind him dressed in black, it was the black mask that caused him to flinch.

"Oh, shit!" Cream shouted.

As if time seemed to slow down, Cream's body leaned to the side just as the gun clapped and the slug went into the window of the passenger's door, causing it to shatter. Cream went down to the pavement. Their guns were inside the truck, so he couldn't return fire. On the other side of the SUV, Ace was trying desperately to get the door open so that he could get to his gun. While at the same time trying to duck and avoid being hit.

Cream's basic instinct kicked in and since he didn't have a gun. He made a crawling scramble around the Denali and then around another car. Somehow, he had a feeling that the person with the gun was behind him, and close. Cream paused by the tire of the car. He glanced around but didn't see anyone. He couldn't even see Ace. He decided to do the smart thing and scooted under the car to hide.

$$$$

Ace managed to get the door open, but for him to get inside to get his gun. He would have to expose himself. That meant taking a chance. He didn't know where Cream was, but he knew they were both in the same situation. Neither one of them had a gun. Deciding to take a chance Ace leaned up and looked across the hood of the Denali. As soon as he did, slugs pelleted the truck.

Boca! Boca! Boca!

Causing him to duck back down. Whoever the fuck this was, the nigga wasn't that far away. It didn't seem like he was about to let up. He reached up slowly and grasped the door handle, Ace paused a moment, waiting to see if his movements were noticed. When he was sure it wasn't, he opened the door but didn't pull it all the way open yet. A few shots rang out, and he suspected the shooter was shooting at Cream. Thinking that this was his chance to make his move. Ace stood up and made a quick glance around before he pulled the door farther open and he froze.

$$$$

It must have been the dope, Rook thought.

Because it seemed like all his senses were on high alert. As if everything was moving slower than it should have been. When he turned his head to look around, he thought he'd seen this nigga Cream moving over in the other direction. So, he wasn't expecting to see this other nigga trying to get into the truck.

Rook couldn't believe how fast he moved. It had to be the dope. One minute he was looking into the niggaz face. Then the hand he held the gun in came up with the quickness. If he didn't know any better, he would have sworn that he was a gunslinger from the wild west days.

Boca! Boca! Boca! Boca!

He introduced slug after slug into this niggaz body and watched in stunned silence as his body danced. Rook was so entranced by the way Ace's body twisted and jerked that he wasn't aware of Cream sneaking up on him.

$$$$

Cream knew that he couldn't save Ace. He too took a chance on standing and taking a peek. When he did, he happened to catch the beginning when the person in the ski-mask locked in on Ace and started shooting. The distance between himself and the shooter was too far for him to prevent the inevitable, but he did use the situation to the best of his advantage. Common sense said that running wasn't an option. He would only receive a slug in the back and several more once he went down. Meaning that the only thing he could do was approach the problem.

Mathematical logic said that it would take him at least twenty quiet steps in order to reach the shooter. Especially if he wanted to be undetected. When he moved the shooter was squeezing off his second shot. Cream didn't know how many rounds he was going to send into Ace's body. He moved around two cars, in between another car and a van. Cream was right behind the shooter just as the gun went empty.

"Shit," the shooter cursed.

"I would have said *fuck* if I were you," Cream said. "Because you're about to get fucked over." As soon as the shooter heard his voice, he turned to face him.

However, that didn't work out good for him at all. Cream had been a fighter way before he picked up his first pistol. The way he grew up in Brooklyn, was fighting neighborhood bullies just about every day. He wasn't allowed to run. His mother wouldn't have understood him running. So, he learned to stand his ground. In doing so, his fight game eventually became legendary.

Cream caught the shooter with a nice left hook to his temple that was followed with a right jab. The shooter dropped the gun and stumbled backward. Cream watched as the shooter brought both hands up as if to guard his grill. Something didn't quite seem right. Either way, he didn't stop to ask questions. He continued to throw and deliver punch after punch. While the shooter's body moved like it was a bobblehead. Then Cream drew back, thoughts of this guy killing Ace played in his head.

Cream swung, with all his strength, and connected with the right side of the shooter's head. The blow within itself was all it took to knock the guy out. Cream watched as his body went down. He stood there and glanced around. He didn't see anyone else out in the parking lot. Nor did he hear any police sirens in the distance.

Cream squatted next to the body and reached to remove the ski-mask. "Ain't this a bitch?" he said as he looked down into Rook's unconscious face.

$$$$

Vanessa didn't know what to think about the phone call. On one hand, it didn't make any sense. She even tried to rationalize that the nigga might be on some freaky shit, which was why she made it a point to put on the wrap-around dress that was made by Prada. Minus a certain pair of lace panties. Just in case this nigga was on some super tough shit. Because as she maneuvered her car until she found the road that led to the underside of the Sandbar Ferry Bridge. She still couldn't understand why Cream wanted her to meet him under the bridge, and as she checked the time on her Dior watch. Seeing that it was nearly midnight, but she found the road and flicked on her high beams. Vanessa drove about a quarter of a mile until she saw Cream standing next to a dark blue Ford Explorer that didn't really look like it was his style.

She pulled up alongside it and parked. Then she exited her Benz. "Nigga—" that was the first word out of her mouth as she got out of the car. "I know you didn't call me way out here to get yo freak on?" Vanessa walked over to where he stood with his back against the Explorer. She saw that a small area of a window was broken and then her expression changed. "I was just about to ask you where your Escalade was. Nigga you must be doing some dirt, riding around in hot boxes and shit?" she stated.

Vanessa watched as he casually smiled at her. "Come here I need to show you something," he said.

She followed as he walked around to the back of the truck. Vanessa waited while he opened the back and lowered the tailgate. That's when she saw Rook laying on his side. His hands and feet were bound with duct tape and a piece across his mouth. He looked like a pig about to be roasted.

"Ha." She laughed. "Looks like you beat his ass. He must've gotten disrespectful."

Vanessa turned to look into Cream's face, and she saw that he wasn't smiling. Instead, he had a deadly serious look on his face. "What did he do?" she asked.

Realizing this was far more serious than a fight.

"All I need to know is do you love this nigga?" he asked.

She watched as he reached into his waistband and removed the Glock .22. He dug into his pocket and brought out a 3 ½ inch silencer which he screwed onto the barrel.

That's when she finally understood that whatever Rook had done, Cream wasn't about to spare his life.

Vanessa looked down into Rook's face. She saw that his eyes were locked on the gun. She could see the fear and when he noticed that she was watching him, Rook turned pleading eyes to her.

"Emotions ain't got nothing to do with violations," she stated. "Business is business, that shit ain't personal."

She had a feeling that Cream was in some type of way trying her. Yet, she watched as he looked into her eyes as if searching for something. There ain't nothing between me and this nigga except my daughter," she stated.

This nigga just tried to kill me," Cream said.

He watched as her emotions changed. That was the thing about Vanessa. Her emotions seemed to be controlled like a light switch. One minute she could be in a good mood. Laughing and smiling, then the switch gets flipped and she's on the bullshit. He watched her look down at Rook.

"He killed Ace instead. I just wanted to see what this nigga meant to you before I dead his ass," Cream explained.

Vanessa realized he must be waiting on her to say something. "What?" she asked. "

You don't wanna ask me to spare his life because of your daughter?" he asked. "You know so she can grow up knowing her father?"

"Pissh." She blew out between her teeth. "Toiya will be alright. Don't let that stop you from handling yo' business."

Cream couldn't help but smile. Because he knew that there was no saving this nigga. He'd just wanted to see how she would take it and her response told him exactly what he needed to know.

$$$$

It didn't take long for the truck to sink in the Savannah River. Once the top of it went under the water, both of them got into Vanessa's Benz and drove away. Neither one of them were even looking back. Rook was no longer a part of either one of their lives. That was only a chapter in her life that had ended. Vanessa gave it no more thought. Cream was glad that she didn't get into her feelings about the nigga. As she drove, he thought about Young Castro's phrase.

He looked over and said. "I like the way you do business." He watched as she sucked her teeth and smiled.

Chapter Seventeen

Young Castro sat on the other side of the table and listened along with everyone else as Cream explained the whole situation to all of them. At least this time they knew who did the killing. They were all seated inside the club on Mike Padgett Highway called Magic City. Jeeta as usual sat next to him texting back and forth with Crystal. Young knew that he heard every word that was spoken. Poe sat next to Cream on the other side of the table. He hadn't said much himself.

"Listen, Son, it's gon' be hard for me to put it down the way you want it without a right hand," Cream explained. He looked straight at Young. "You've got a lot of food on the table, bruh, and only two teams."

"So, what are you suggesting, Pah?" Young asked.

"We need another captain, bruh. It would only make sense if you bump D-block up," Cream stated.

When he made the statement, Young noticed the way Jeeta glanced sideways at him. Probably because he'd also hinted at the same thing. "You think D-Block can handle that much product?" he asked.

"I do," Poe said.

Everyone looked at him, even Jeeta. "Yo', on some real nigga shit," Poe began. "Not only does she have a nice team with her sister. You know blood is thicker than water. And none of them bitches play games. But she also got the young God behind her."

He was referring to Damian because they all knew that the streets were afraid of Damien for some reason. It was like him and his partner Justice had the *boo* on everybody. They didn't even sell drugs. The only thing people knew of them for in Augusta, was a few conflicts that were about D-Block.

"I gotta agree wit' you cuz," Jeeta put in. "At first, I thought that it was a bad idea. We all know how D-Block can get into her feelings at times, but you're right. Ain't many niggaz gon' try her either. Especially with that nigga Damian being around."

Young Castro processed all the information he'd just heard. Both he and Jeeta needed to get started on this car business ASAP. The first shipment arrived a few days ago, and those were sitting inside a storage warehouse that he'd leased. Plus, they still had these ATF and DEA officials to worry about. They could not be made into a RICO case.

"A'ight, Pah," Young began. "Me and Jeeta gon' pull up on D-Block and see if she'll accept the job. But in the meantime, Poe, how you coming with the shop?"

He watched as Poe took a moment to think about it. So, far he'd only been the owner a few days, but he knew how to run everything because of all the time they'd spent hanging with Young at the shop.

"Yo, we good, son?" Poe began. "I'm not making any major changes. I am putting my name up over that muthafucka, though." He laughed.

"No doubt, Pah, do you." Young laughed too, then turned his attention to Cream. "What about you, Pah?" he asked, then watched as Cream sighed heavily.

"On the one, bruh. Shit is on hold until I can get my house in order," he stated, looking somewhat confused as he spoke. "If I make that legal play right now, my pockets gon' suffer."

"I smell you, Pah. Business is business," Young Castro said and paused to think about something. "What happened to that little bloody nigga that Ace was talking about putting on? What was his name?"

"Shine," Cream told him.

"Yeah, Shine," Young stated. "What about him? Can you use him?" he asked.

Cream took time to think about the situation. In truth, he knew Shine. He knew enough to know that for him to be so young his hustle game was nice. So, he made the conscious decision to look into him.

$$$$

"Just one time—just one." D-Block looked around the kitchen. She was standing inside the lab, where her cooks turned the cocaine into crack and cut it up into what it would be needed for. At the moment she was looking around at her six workers and she wasn't happy. "Can I just come over here once and not have to deal with somebody's bullshit?" she asked.

Her workers were complaining about the extra work since she was getting a larger product now. They were asking for more money. D-Block rolled her eyes when she looked over at Niecy, her head girl. She was thirty-two, had three kids, and lived in the projects. Niecy was claiming to need more money because of her situation. Ironically, all the workers were women, and they all had children.

"A'ight." D-Block sighed. "I'ma give everybody a raise. And you bitches betta fuckin' appreciate it, too."

She stood there and watched as they all celebrated and high-fived one another. She would have said more, but her phone rang, and when she pulled it out to answer. Diane saw that it was Young Castro's number on the screen.

The fuck? she thought, then answered. "Yeah, what's up?"

"Ayo, Peace Ma. You busy?" Young asked.

"Not really, just checking on my lab. Why is something going on that I need to know about?"

"Actually, Ma I just spoke wit' yo better half. I need to meet with both of you at your earliest convenience," Young said.

He spoke with Damian, she thought. Wondering what that could be about.

"Well, if I've got to bring Brina and Nessa I'm not sure what would be a good time," she said.

"Nah, nah, Ma. Just you and Pah," he told her.

"What did Damian say?" She was curious now.

She still didn't understand the so-called communication between Young Castro and Damian. Her baby's father wasn't forthcoming about it either. Something else she had to look into.

"Son said we can do it in about an hour if you ain't busy. So, if it's good wit' you. How about we meet at the Riverwalk in like forty-five minutes?" he stated.

"I can do forty-five, let me hit my nigga and see what's up," she stated.

Young Castro ended the call. *What the fuck was that about,* she thought as she went to her contacts and dialed Damian's number.

"Peace, Queen. What's your science?" he answered. "You told Young we could meet him tonight." She made it a question, not a statement. On the other end of the phone, she could hear what sounded like Damian inhaling.

"Huh—what?" he asked as if his lungs were filled and she shook her head.

"Young Castro, nigga we meeting him in thirty minutes. So, get yo head right. Meet me at the Riverwalk," she stated.

"A'ight—I'ma be there." He inhaled.

Diane ended the call. She still couldn't understand how this nigga did half the shit that he did in the streets. Ninety percent of the time he was higher than a Whitney Houston high note.

She shook the thought off and slid the phone back into her pocket. Again she tried to figure out what Young Castro wanted.

$$$$

This might just work, Juanita thought as she sat inside of the dark grey Q7 Audi.

She thought that with Ace being killed her plan wasn't going to work. Having invested so much time into learning most of his habits. When word came that someone tried to kill Cream and in return killed his partner. She almost didn't believe it. When reality set in, she was about to give up on the whole thing. Then something made her go back to the area where Ace had hustled. At first, she didn't understand why. She really couldn't see a reason for her being there. After about ten minutes of sitting there in the shadows. She saw the cream-colored Escalade SRX all-wheel drive, sitting on the RBP Blade custom satin black diamond-cut rims. The SUV pulled up and she knew whose it was as soon as she saw it. Juanita was actually about to leave until that moment. So, she decided to wait and see what would happen.

$$$$

Cream let the window down and looked out at Ace's trap. He saw the young soldier Shine out giving instructions to what were now *his* workers. As he sat there thinking about it. Cream realized that Shine might actually be a good man for the job. Already, he was stepping up and filling in Ace's shoes. Cream thought unless he had someone else backing him. The little nigga must've brought some dope of his own. Which would make him a very smart brother to take advantage of the vacancy left by Ace.

Cream leaned out of the window part way. "Ayo— Shine." He whistled and watched as Shine turned to look. He held up a finger, then finished his instructions to the three younger hustlers. *Shine can't be any older than nineteen maybe twenty,* he thought.

Once he finished speaking, Shine turned and walked over toward him. "What that be about, Thug?" Shine asked.

Cream smiled, his fashion didn't at all stand out, but it would be impossible for someone not to recognize him as a Blood. Shine stood there in True' Religion blue jeans, a 5XL Iceberg jersey that was a deep dark red, and the dark red Timberlands all color Euro's with the bubblegum soles.

"You look like you're busy." Cream smiled as he nodded to where the three younger hustlers were now putting in work.

Shine smiled with pride. "Yeah, wit' bruh gone. Shit somebody had to step their game up. So, I figured, why shouldn't it be me." Now he was beaming.

"No doubt. No doubt, youngsta," Cream said. He glanced around real quick.

"Look," he added. "You got time to take this ride around the block and back? I've got some shit I wanna run by you."

"Yeah, we can do that," Shine said.

$$$$

Juanita watched the whole play from a distance. She knew that the young guy was one of Ace's workers. Having observed them upon several occasions. At which times she never gave him much attention. After all, he was young. She didn't think that he was old enough to purchase beer yet. She also knew that he wasn't a child either. So, as she watched him get into the SUV with Cream and they left. Juanita was contemplating a new plan. Common sense told her that Cream's visit was about business. It didn't take much for her to put the pieces together, with both Juggernaut and Ace gone. Cream would need to fill in the void and the next person in line to move up would be this young guy.

The question to her was, could she seduce this young hustler and gain control over him. Because if she could, then she would still be able to get into Young Castro's inner circle. She still needed them to do something about Hernandez before she could take control of the Hispanic Community. Then she could get rich.

$$$$

"You see, Pah, I don't think we gon' have to worry about them DEA muthafuckaz. Shit, we've got the car show muthafucka up and running and that's legal," Young Castro said between bites.

Both he and Jeeta were standing at the banister looking out into the waters of the Savannah River. Jeeta as usual held his phone in one hand and what was left of a blunt in the other. While Young Castro stood there eating honey-roasted peanuts.

"Especially with, big bruh getting his future father in law to help us out," he added.

Francis eventually went to Lloyd, Jazmine's father, and the ADA of Richmond County. As a favor, Lloyd pulled some strings and helped them get official papers for the building they were using. Making everything legal.

"So, all we gotta do is make sure we keep our books in order. Keep everything looking clean and we ain't got no problems, Pah," Young was saying.

Then he looked up when he saw the tall, handsome, clean-cut brother in the jeans and T-shirt walking toward them. Next to him was the beautiful Diane Blaylock, looking like she should have been a model instead of a thug.

"My nigga," Damian stated as he approached. Then he and Young Castro hugged like old friends. When they parted, Damian gave Jeeta some dap.

"What's good, baby?" Young said, then looked at Diane.

"Muthafuckin,' D-Block. What's up, baby? Damn you get finer every time I see you." He embraced her briefly.

"Whatever, nigga. You know I've got this bullshit detector in my back pocket right," she stated.

"Slow yo roll, Ma. This ain't no beef. We all civilized out here." He laughed.

Then Young Castro glanced around to make sure there weren't any people close enough to hear what he was about to say.

"Listen, D, I need yo help. Seriously," he stated and watched as she looked him up and down. "Nigga." She looked over to where Jeeta had stopped texting and seemed to be paying attention.

"I thought you niggaz didn't need no help killing niggaz?" She jokingly said,

"Stop playing, ma." Young laughed. "I actually don't want you to kill nobody else unless it's absolutely necessary. And even then I'd rather you let this nigga do it instead." He nodded to Damian. D-Block sucked her teeth and rolled her eyes. "Nah, ma, seriously you make too much noise when yo heat go off. But yo' mans—yo, Pah is still the best-kept secret in Augusta, right now," he stated.

No one argued the point, because both him and Jeeta knew some of what Damian and his partner Justice did.

"So, what exactly do you need me to do?" Diane asked.

"I need you to step up, ma," Young Castro stated outright. "My team has gotten smaller. I'm trying to duck these DEA muthafuckaz who on some type of homo shit. And me and Pah got a business to run. So, I need you, seriously, ma."

Now Diane looked confused. Her eye's shifted from Young Castro to Jeeta. Then she looked at Damian, who was trying to act nonchalant about the whole thing which made her suspect that he already knew what was going on.

"Okay, so what you need me to do?" she asked.

They all stood there and listened while Young Castro outlined what he needed her to do. Before he and Jeeta left, she'd agreed to be his fourth Lieutenant and turn her physical activities down a notch or two.

Trai'Quan

Chapter Eighteen

Brooklyn, New York

Present

Jameen stepped inside of the club feeling like he was New York City's favorite son. Wearing True Religion jeans, a nice Fred Perry shirt, and Marsey dress shoes. On his wrist, he flexed a nice Cartier watch that seemed to speak its own language every time the light struck the face of it.

"The fuck this nigga Kingston at?" he mumbled.

Kingston was an Island nigga that he'd met a little over a month ago. In that time Jameen had been trying to get him to sell him some major weight. But sometimes it seemed like these Island niggaz were talking funny.

Jameen felt the phone vibrate in his pocket, so he reached in and pulled it out. When he looked he saw Kingston's number.

"Yo' Son, I'm in the club. Where you at?" Jameen asked.

"Calm down, Mon. I up top, look to your left," Kingston told him.

When Jameen turned, he looked up and saw what looked like the VIP section. Through the glass window and even from that distance. He couldn't miss the large marijuana leaf platinum necklace. That was known as Kingston's trademark throughout Brooklyn.

"Yeah, yeah, I smell you, son. I'm on my way up." Jameen ended the call.

Then he proceeded to make his way through the crowded club to the stairs. He really needed this thing with these niggaz to go right. Because his hustle game hadn't been right since he did that bid at Clinton. When he came home it seemed like niggaz had forgotten that he was ever in the streets and nobody was around to show love. He heard it before he left the Island that Young Castro came back to New York and scooped some niggaz up.

Prophet still couldn't believe that he'd lost control of that lil nigga. But he should have known when he found out Needle fucked up the lick. After that, he hadn't seen nor heard from the lil nigga. Until his sister told him the nigga was down South. As far as she knew, the nigga was getting money.

At the door, Jameen was let into the booth, which was actually an office with nice comfortable furniture in it. He saw a few bitches drinking Ciroc and smoking blunts. He already knew that these weren't exactly the type of bitches he fucked with. Even though they were fine, Jameen knew each one of them were soldiers in Kingston's army.

Meaning, they'd suck your dick and cut your throat all at the same time. He saw the tall, dark-skinned dreadlock wearing Jamaican standing near the window. Kingston held what looked like the biggest blunt in the world. Jameen watched as he inhaled the thick smoke that he drew from it.

"Bum da clot," Kingston exclaimed. Then his eyes came to rest on Jameen. "Der im is da Prophet im self. Ow yer feel, Mon?"

Jameen smiled as he approached. "Yo, yo, I'm good, baby. I'm good." They clasp hands a moment, then Kingston passed Jameen the extra-large blunt.

"Ere fill yer lungs, Mon. Smoke up," Kingston stated.

He watched as Jameen brought the blunt to his lips and inhaled deeply. "Yo'" he choked. "Yo', that shit right there. That shit'll kill Jesus," Jameen stated.

He laughed along with Kingston as he passed the blunt back. The weed had to be good. Because as Kingston led him over to the couch, Jameen hadn't paid any attention to the way the older man watched him.

$$$$

Kingston didn't know why Big Dredd wanted him to keep this snake close to him? But an order was an order, for whatever reason Big Dredd called and asked him to set up an operation in Flatbush. Kingston just did it. Then Big Dredd sent him a name. Kingston found out who the individual was. He told Big Dredd that this was a shiesty one and that he would be trying his best not to kill him.

When he first met Jameen the Prophet, he could see the poison in him right off. Then when he checked in with some of the other Rastas that had been in Brooklyn for some time. He heard all the stories about how Jameen was a black devil. Even now, as he looked at the man. Kingston felt the hairs on his arms stand up. This Prophet Jameen was pure evil.

Nevertheless, Big Dredd said keep him close. This was a favor for someone else. Kingston wondered if death would be the outcome. Because instincts were telling him that Brooklyn would be better off without this evil.

$$$$

Augusta, GA

"We're going to need some help on this, Pah," Young Castro stated.

He was talking to Jeeta. Who just happened to be seated over in the passenger seat? They were both in the dark grey Mazda CX7, which was parked up the street from where Hernandez's people ran their business.

"It's not that we can't get these niggaz ourselves. But we'll need to do it all at the same time," he explained.

The plan was to take out Hernandez and his immediate circle which consisted of about ten other MS-13s. While they were doing that, Money-Loc and his crew needed to be taken care of. He'd already told Jeeta they would see him coming a mile away.

"So, if I don't hit Money -Loc and his boys. Then who gon' do it? I thought you wanted to keep Poe and Cream in the open so the DEA could keep watching them?" Jeeta outlined.

Young Castro watched Hernandez sit up on the hood of his CTS-V Coupe. He held a young Mexican female by the hips as he talked to her.

"Yeah, you right Son," Young Castro said. "We can get these cornballs ass niggaz ourselves. It shouldn't take more than me and you. Look at these niggaz, Pah," he said.

Jeeta watched, the whole scene was lazy. Mostly because this area of Central Avenue only consisted of Mexicans. Over time it seemed they'd brought or leased every house on this side street. There was a handful that they didn't own that the Mexicans were calling Baby Mexico.

Only a fool would try to run up in their spot on bullshit. So, they hung out, sold dope, and got drunk. It didn't look like they were worried about anything. Not on their street anyway.

"Yo'—these muthafuckaz won't expect it. They seem to always have their guards down," Young said.

They watched as an argument seemed to break out between a few other Mexicans. There were girls out there as well. Some of them even looked like they might be gang banging.

"A'ight, so what about Money?" Jeeta asked.

Young Castro turned to look at him. "I already got somebody on it. All it'll take is a phone call," he explained.

Jeeta thought about it. He knew that with Young Castro it was nearly impossible to know his every move unless he told you about it. He really couldn't worry about that, right now. At the moment he had to get his thoughts together. Because this was about to go down now. Jeeta watched as Young pulled his phone out.

$$$$

Justice looked over from the driver's seat when he heard the phone ring. He watched as Damian barely glanced down at the phone. Instead, he continued to watch the streets. At the moment they were parked two blocks up from where Money-Loc and his crew hustled.

"It's about that time ain't it?" Justice asked.

"No doubt." Damian reached into the backseat and lifted the M-4 Assault rifle.

The M-4 he held was specially modified and shot both semi and fully automatic. Each clip held twenty-one rounds. To prevent a burn out the gun was made with an 18-inch stainless barrel that also had a cooler built onto it. He checked the clip and made sure that the safety wasn't on.

He looked over to Justice. "Yo' you ready to get this money?" he asked.

Justice lit the Newport that had been hanging out of the left corner of his mouth. Then lifted his Glock 9mm off his lap.

"Let's get it, baby."

$$$$

Money sat on the hood of the royal blue Chrysler 300 SRT Sedan that he hadn't been too long brought. He liked the car, it was big and extremely comfortable. Money watched as C-Loc, Lil Snoop, Tru-Loc, and Jay-Loc played Cee-Lo. He didn't gamble himself. Money-Loc liked to make money and spend it, not donate it to foolishness. As he sat there, he watched as it seemed Jay-Loc was taking the three younger fools to school. Him being originally from New Jersey, it seemed like he was born with a set of dice clutched in his palm. Money was thinking, even if he did gamble, he wouldn't play with Jay-Loc. That in itself seemed stupid. Either way, he had other shit on his mind.

The streets had been quiet since someone tried to make it look like they killed Juggernaut. Some shit that he highly suspected Hernandez was behind. He couldn't prove it, and even if he could. There wasn't anything he could do. Hernandez was his source for product. If he did something about the disrespect, they would lose what they had. Right now, they were making $10,000.00 a week. Whereas, before they were barely pulling in four grand a week. Hernandez made it where they could step up and Money was enjoying the move.

On the other hand, he didn't have any love for Jeeta and them niggaz he worked with. Which meant he really didn't care, as long as nobody was pushing up on his spot.

$$$$

"What? This nigga ain't answering my call?" Diane looked down at her iPhone as if it were the enemy or something.

Having just tried to call Damian and he didn't pick up, which was something he wouldn't do unless he was doing something else that was important. She turned her Infiniti QX56 into Apple Valley and began to slow down.

"The fuck this nigga at?" she spoke out loud.

She really didn't want to be out this way by herself, looking for any nigga. Let alone this nigga Maine. She drove up one street, then turned on the next. That's when she saw the large Forest green F-250 with the Chrome Pinnacle rims on it. In front of the truck there stood a group of guys. She couldn't tell much, but it looked like they were watching something.

Diane pulled up and parked behind the truck then stepped out. Because she didn't know how this would play out. She had worn a pair of jeans by Robert Cavalli and Timberland Euros the sky-blue dyed kind, with her starter jacket on, it was easy to conceal her Glock .40.

She knew Maine from high school, but that was a long time ago for her. Some of the things she'd been hearing in the streets were suggesting that he was far more mentally healthy now than he'd been then. As she walked up to the crowd, Diane saw just what they meant. Lying on the street looking like Wolverine had just cut him ten times, was a fairly large-sized man. He had to have been about 6'5 and over 300lbs. It looked like he'd just fought an animal of some kind that was larger than him. The only threat Diane could see was 5'11 and no more than 190lbs. Maine stood there over the fallen man, holding a large knife in one hand, and breathing hard.

"Pussy ass nigga," Maine cursed. "Done made me fuck up my suit."

It was at that point Diane realized he was wearing what looked like an expensive two-piece Armani suit. There was blood on it and what she thought was a knife was actually a straight razor.

"Get this nigga outta here," he stated.

She watched as others began to lift the big man and dragged him toward one of the houses. While someone else handed Maine a towel. He tried to clean his hands, then looked around and smiled when he saw her.

"Well, if it ain't, Little Dye—aka to the streets nowadays, D-Block?" he called out.

He approached and leaned down to give her a light hug, trying not to get any blood on her. "Girl, I heard you was terrorizing them niggaz downtown?" He laughed.

"Pissh." Diana stepped back and looked him up and down. "Nigga, you look more like the Middle East terrorist to me. Out here cutting up motherfuckaz and shit."

Maine laughed and around them the crowd disbursed. "Nah, just tightening up an old disrespect. Shit, I've been in control of my temper lately." He smiled. Diane swore it looked evil and sneaky. "So, what brings you uptown?" he asked.

Chapter Nineteen

"Boy, you know you lying," Gloria stated blushing.

She stood two feet away from where Hernandez sat on the hood of his car. Profiling, trying to look like he was really advertising it. While trying to run his game on her. She knew it was all game. Just like she knew he wasn't anywhere near serious about talking to her. Gloria knew his only goal was to fuck her. Especially knowing that she was one of the small handful of women he hadn't had sex with on their street.

"Nah, baby, you giving that shit too much thought. I'm just trying to spend some time with you," Hernandez explained. "It ain't even got to be nothing serious."

Yeah, right, she thought.

Here she was an average plain Jane and him, the big Jefe' who ran all the MS-13s in Augusta. All his money, expensive clothes and cars and he was trying to convince her that he was being serious.

Gloria was just about to tell him that she might be young, but far from stupid. Only when she started to form the words, her eyes caught movement. When she focused on it, Gloria became aware of the fact that two black guys were walking up their street, which was more than off. Because the Mexicans now owned more than 65% of the houses on their street. There weren't many blacks left and those that were, everybody knew them. Yet, she'd never seen these two guys before. Just as that thought began to register, so too did the fact that both men held guns.

"Uh, Hernandez," she mumbled.

He turned to look behind him, as he completed the turning motion, Hernandez realized that he'd been caught down bad. He didn't have his gun on him. It was inside the car because he hadn't expected any trouble. He was just trying to get his dick wet. All of a sudden, when he actually realized who the two niggers were. Instincts took over, and he gave a war cry in Spanish. No sooner had he given the word, and push Gloria to the side, the gunfight began.

$$$$

Young Castro didn't even wait to see what Jeeta would do. Instead, he dove behind one of the cars that were parked along the street. Then he leaned sideways and began taking aim at the Mexican dope dealers that were shooting at them. He heard the sounds of Jeeta's guns not far away, so he knew he was alright.

The mission objective was to kill the nigga Hernandez. Young leaned forward and looked around the car, he saw several of the so-called soldiers standing in the middle of the street shooting. They seemed to be aiming at the cars they hid behind. It didn't look like any of them were putting any serious effort into their shooting. Young realized they were either high or drunk, which meant focus was affected.

He let off a few more shots with the 9mm, putting down two of the Mexicans. When the clip emptied, he dropped the gun to the street. Young wasn't worried about fingerprints because they wore latex gloves and all of the guns, they were using tonight had been cleaned. He reached into the back of his jeans and pulled the .44 Desert Eagles and came up shooting.

$$$$

Jeeta stepped from behind the minivan that he'd ducked behind. When he saw Young Castro come up with both guns in hand, he knew it was time to get serious. So, he brought the

12 gauge up and sent a shell in the chamber. When he squeezed the trigger, the shotgun seemed to speak with the voice of the Lord.

Boom! Kha! Chink! Boom!

Because he was using scattered shots, every shot sent two or more bodies down, with a gun like this on deck, the worst thing to do would be to stand close together.

At the moment, Jeeta wasn't sparing anything in the streets. If they were still standing when he cocked a shell into the chamber. They were falling once he pulled the trigger. It was just that simple. This was the business for tonight.

$$$$

Juanita sat further up the street and watched as it all went down. She hated that so many of her own people had to die tonight. But these were her brother's soldiers. His elite, those who stood next to him. She really wouldn't need any of them for her plans anyway. In fact, it was a good thing that Young Castro was cleaning the trash for her.

As she sat there, she watched Hernandez as he retrieved his gun from inside the car. Now he was crouched behind the car returning shots. What surprised her the most was that Hernandez hadn't turned and ran yet. He'd never been a soldier himself. One of the main reasons they'd moved here was because he couldn't get ahead in Texas.

The Mexicans there wouldn't follow him like the Mexicans here did. Hernandez had money, but he didn't have the street credibility needed to be a real JeFe, Boss. So, when he found Augusta and moved here. He made it a point to only move those Mexicans who were loyal to money. Those who could buy these were the Mexicans who originally moved to Central Avenue. Others moved there later, from other areas.

Juanita watched as Young Castro and his right-hand moved through the streets killing. She was impressed by their level of intensity. These guys were serious. The shootout lasted less than twenty minutes. She watched as the last of her brother's soldiers decided to turn and run. Then she watched as Hernandez must've come to the same conclusion. He turned himself and ran.

"Fuck," she cursed.

$$$$

Young Castro stood in the middle of the street and watched as Hernandez ran. Jeeta came to stand next to him.

"We might not be able to catch him tonight," Jeeta said as he pushed new shells into the shotgun.

"Yeah, it looks that way, Pah," Young stated.

They stood watching as Hernandez glanced over his shoulder, running up the street. They could probably catch him if they pushed the issue. Then again, with his whole crew dead, Hernandez was nothing. Young was just about to say this when they saw a car further up the street start. The lights came on and flashed twice. Hernandez must have noticed. Because he made his way to the car's passenger door. They watched as whoever was inside the car fired two shots into Hernandez.

"Ain't that a bitch?" Jeeta said.

Then watched as the body fell to the street and the car turned in the street. Then it picked up speed leaving Hernandez's body lying there.

"I wonder who that could have been, son?" Young Castro stated.

"It really doesn't matter. The muthafucka is dead. Come on let's get outta here before the cops show up," Jeeta said.

182

They turned to leave. Young pulled his phone out and sent a quick text. When they reached the car, he received a text.

"Yo', them niggaz Money-Loc and his crew got touched, too," Young told him. They got in the car, with Jeeta behind the wheel.

"Alright, so this is the beginning. Now, where do we go from here?" Jeeta asked.

He started the car and pulled away from the street they'd done all of the killings on. Young Castro was quiet. He was in thinking mode.

"I don't know who was in that ride, Pah. But it looks like they had beef wit' that nigga and not us. If that's the case, then we should be good on this end," Young outlined.

"That seems logical. So, we focus on this car dealership and get out of the spotlight?" Jeeta said.

"Not quite," Young said as he sat in the passenger seat looking out the window. He was watching the streets, the lights, and the other cars go by.

His mind was on something else or rather someone else at the moment. He'd asked Big Dredd to get someone to watch Jameen's movements for him. Big Dredd wanted to know why. So, he had to explain the situation. Once he'd told Big Dredd the truth, the older man suggested that Young let him send someone to take care of Jameen.

However, Young had explained that this was a personal issue. Something that he had to do on his own. Big Dredd said he respected that. So, Young knew of Jameen's every move now.

"I gotta take a quick trip back home," Young said as he still gazed out the window. "Got some business I need to attend to in Brooklyn."

"I can go with you if you need me to," Jeeta said.

"Nah, Pah, you gotta keep the business down here in its fit formation. I can handle this," he said and he would.

$$$$

"Excuse me, Jefe, I'm trying to find some good green to smoke. Can you help me?"

Shine looked at the car as the woman spoke through the window. Unlike the other two niggaz walking with him. He knew what the word Jefe' meant. So, he stopped and faced the car. From what he could see, the woman was beautiful. Since she sounded Hispanic, he'd already assumed she was Mexican.

"Damn, Mami, it's kinda late to be out here looking for some weed. You could have sent your man out to do that for you." Shine smiled.

"Assuming I have a man right?" Juanita asked. "Baby, as good as you look. It would be a shame if you don't," he said. "But I don't have any weed on me, baby."

"That's cute. How old are you?" she asked.

He'd already figured out she was older than him by more than ten years. "I'm twenty, I'll be twenty-one month after next," he said.

Juanita smiled seductively. "So, uh," she began.

"Shine." She looked at his friends.

"So, Shine, would you happen to know where I can find some good green?" she asked.

"Yeah, but it's not within walking distance. And no offense, I don't know you, lady."

"That's cool. If you don't feel comfortable riding with me. Then you can just tell me where to go. I'm quite sure I can find it," she explained.

Then she waited as he appeared to be thinking about it.

Shine looked back at his two workers. They'd really already discussed business. It wasn't like he had to be in the house at a certain time. His moms never said anything as long as he paid half of the bills.

"Look, I'ma catch-up wit' you niggaz tomorrow. Just remember what I said." He walked around the car then open the passenger door to get in. Shine's eyes fell directly on her thighs which were shown because her skirt seemed to have ridden up on them. He closed the door. "You know my name, Mami, but I don't know yours."

She smiled. "You can call me, Anita. So, where are we going?"

"Oh, we gotta go to the bottom. I know somebody down in River Glenn got that good-good," he told her."

Juanita put the car into drive and pulled off. Seeing as she no longer had to worry about Hernandez. She decided to go ahead with her plans. The most important part of those plans was being able to get inside of Young Castro's structure some type of way. To get in without them suspecting something.

"So, Shine, you're out here running the streets with your boys. You don't have a girl to get home to?"

"Nah, I been too busy trying to get my business right. Ain't had time for no girls," he explained.

"What no baby mama's or nothing?" she asked.

He shook his head. "You're not uh, gay, are you?"

Shine looked at her thighs and then up into her face. "Baby, ain't nothing about me funny. And I don't mind proving it," he stated.

Juanita smiled. *Oh, we gon' see,* she thought. *We gon' definitely see.*

Chapter Twenty

The Junkie rolled over and tried to get comfortable. The blanket that he pulled up over himself seemed to have so many holes in it that it really wasn't doing much to keep the chill off. That was the reason he was having trouble getting to sleep. It was bad enough the abandoned building already housed several others. On his floor alone there were thirteen others. None of these bastards were trying to share. He hadn't had a good hit of the boy in two days. The crack he smoked didn't seem to do what he wanted.

"Hey, ole man. You got a second?"

The Junkie turned his head up and looked at the man standing over him. He must've either been too cold, or the crack was still in his system. Because he hadn't even noticed the guy walking up.

"What—" He coughed. "What can I do for you?" The Junkie asked eye level with him. The Junkie could have sworn he knew the guy from somewhere.

"You don't remember me, do you?" The younger man asked.

"No—no I don't think so," The Junkie said. "Do I owe you some money or something?"

"Nah, but your name is Coogi, right?"

The Junkie smiled. "It used to be when I was a booster back in the day." Coogi stopped talking and looked closer at the younger man. "Hey, is you Sonya's lil boy—uh—uh." He couldn't grasp the name.

"Casey." Young Castro smiled. "Yeah, that's me."

"Damn, son, I sho am sorry about what happened to your ma. I didn't know, I swear," Coogi said.

"You wanna tell me what happened?" Young asked.

He watched as Coogi looked at him confused. "You—you didn't know?" he asked.

Young shook his head. "I heard something a little while ago. But I don't know what's true or lies."

"It was the Prophet," Coogi stated he watched as Young nodded his head. "He lied to us. Had us boost some shit then he wouldn't pay. And Sonya—" Coogi's voice failed. "She-she offered to take care of him. But he laughed an evil laugh like the devil. So, she said her son's old man was a cop and she was gon' go to him about it—" Coogi paused in his re-telling. "Prophet didn't know, but I knew. The old man wasn't a cop in New York. But she kept talking as if he was. So, Prophet, he gave us the dope. I thought it was to shut her up. So, we went back to her apartment to get high."

Coogi coughed as he sat up a little straighter. "Since it was her dope, I didn't say nothing when she wanted to hit it first—" He paused and looked into Young's eyes. "It happened real fast. So, fast that there was nothing I could do. And later I wanted to do something to Prophet—but—"

He fell silent as Young squatted there listening. This wasn't the version he thought he would hear. Everyone told him it was Coogi that Jameen was trying to kill.

"Hey, did she ever say what my old man's name was? His full name?" he asked.

"You got the same first name. Except you got yo mama's last name." Coogi coughed. "His last name was Jefferson. She used to call him C.J."

Young thought about it. He did remember her mentioning someone named CJ. One of those times when she was high and talking crazy. He stood up and looked down at the Junkie. Young dug into his pocket and pulled out some money. "Listen, Pah, I really appreciate your help. And you don't have to worry about the Prophet. I'm going to take care of him."

He gave Coogi some bills. Coogi looked at the money in his hand, then he looked back up. "Son, you gotta be careful with the Prophet," he said. "You never know what he's gonna do next," he added.

"Don't worry, Pah, I got the Prophet," Young stated. Then he turned and left.

$$$$

He knocked on the door and waited. There was some noise inside, then. "Yeah, who is it?" Nasty's voice called out.

"It's me, Young."

It took a second, he heard the chains on the door rattle. Then the door was open. He saw the same ugly nigga standing in his boxers, a wife-beater, and holding a .44 magnum in his hand. "The fuck. Yo' if it ain't the green nigga."

Nasty reached out and pulled him inside. Then he stuck his head out the door and looked both ways up and down the hallway. Nasty closed the door and turned to face Young.

"Nigga, I thought the devil killed you?"

"Nah, I ain't even been in New York," Young said.

He looked around the apartment, there wasn't much that had changed. The guns were still there. "Mind if I have a seat?" Young asked.

"Shit just find you one." Nasty moved to take his usual seat in the lazy boy. "You look like business been good to you," he said.

Taking in the nice clothes Young wore as he cleared a corner of the couch to sit. "Everything is everything, Pah. How things been in the Rotten Apple?"

"The usual, but I know you ain't here to talk about the City. You wanna know what's up wit' Jameen?" Nasty stated.

Young looked at him curiously. "What makes you say that?" he asked.

"The nigga was looking for you right before he went to Clinton. Then he was asking about you when he came home. You should know, word is you came from under a hit he put on you. And dead the niggaz who came at you." Nasty smiled like a proud dad.

"Wasn't much to it. He sent crackheads at me," Young informed.

"So, you left, and now you back. My thoughts are if it was good where you were at. Then you thinking about revenge now. But here's the thing, Jameen ain't worth it. Especially now," Nasty explained. "Right now, ain't shit going good for him. Every time he thinks he's gotten on, them Blood niggaz run up on him. If it ain't them it's the cops. Yo, that nigga got more issues than a prostitute."

Young thought about that. From what Big Dredd told him that his people knew about Jameen. It was nearly the same information. Jameen was struggling. Either way, he still had a score to settle.

$$$$

"The fuck Kingston thinks he is, a fuckin delivery boy or something," Jameen bitched as he walked up the street carrying a package.

He understood the logic of doing what you had to do in order to get ahead. This nigga Kingston was the muthafucka in power. If he wanted a serious spot on this niggaz team he had to earn it. He knew that, but a delivery boy? How come he couldn't just body a muthafucka. That was the best way to prove a nigga's loyalty. Instead this muthafucka got a nigga running all the way to Flushing just to make a drop.

190

He turned on to the street and then he looked at the address on the piece of paper. Parson Boulevard, he was at the right building. The paper said apartment 18B. Shit, he wasn't even comfortable being out in Flushing N.Y. This wasn't one of his places to hang. In all honesty, it wasn't as grimy as he liked. But he wasn't here on pleasure, this was business. Jameen hefted the package and entered the building.

He saw that one of the elevators was out and the other one appeared to be at the top of the building. He glanced around, then sighed as he decided to take the stairs. This building wasn't as bad as the ones over in Brooklyn or the Bronx. He only saw a few of the Junkies as he stepped inside the stairwell. Around his way, they would be all around the building. Either way, he stepped around a couple of bums as he made his way up.

"Nah, nah—Jesus gon' come back and it's gon' be one day soon."

Jameen paused halfway up the stairs and looked up. He saw another Junkie standing up on the next landing holding a crack pipe in one hand and a lighter in the other one. The crackhead seemed to be having a conversation with the wall in front of him.

"Oh, you don't think Jesus is real do you?" The crackhead seemed to answer himself.

Jameen stood there watching as he spoke. He couldn't say what it was, but for some reason, the whole thing felt funny to him. It was almost as if—

"I tell you what, let's ask another Prophet. See what he says."

Jameen felt the hair stand up on the back of his neck. He reached into his waist for his gun just as the crackhead turned to face him.

$$$$

Justice turned and looked directly into Jameen's eyes as he spoke.

"Tell me Prophet, Jameen. You think Jesus gon' come back to save the people?" he asked.

He watched as Jameen dropped the package and tried to lift his arm with the heavy .357, but it was too late. Both Young Castro and Damien came up off the floor behind Jameen.

Kha! Chink!

Young cocked the Mossburg before he squeezed.

Jameen tried to turn but couldn't figure it all out in time. He knew this was a setup. Damian pulled his .44 Desert Eagle and aimed it. Justice had already pulled his gun and aimed it. There was a pause and in that pause, Jameen saw the eyes of his killer clearly.

"God's been waiting to call you home, bruh," Young said to him as he squeezed.

Kaboom! The Mossburg shouted her name.

Damian and Justice followed suit and opened up right behind it. As they all pumped round after round into Jameen's body they watched as he did a dance that they'd all seen before. The noise in the stairwell was so loud, it was a wonder no one left their apartments to see what was going on. Then again this was still New York and people knew how to mind their business and keep out of yours.

When the shooting stopped, Jameen's body seemed to be pressed into the wall. The .357 slipped from his hand and fell to the floor. They watched as he appeared to be fighting death for a minute.

"Nah, brother," Young Castro said as he cocked the pump again. Placing the last round into the shotgun's chamber.

"Don't cheat yo' self like that. This is a first-class trip, Pah," he stated and brought the pump up.

Kaboom!

They all watched as the slug tore Jameen's head apart leaving only fragments of his skull still connected. Then his body slid down the wall and stopped moving.

"Come on, son. Let's get outta here," Damian said.

They all turned to leave the building. The news about Jameen the Prophet getting hit ran throughout New York. Most people didn't believe it. Others said it was about time. Either way, the one thing that nobody did was wonder out loud who it was that got the drop on Jameen and put him to rest. Because most people didn't even care.

$$$$

Young Castro sat in the back seat of the Range Rover Sport as Justice drove. Both him and Damian sat in the front seat going back and forth about something. He wasn't paying them any attention. Young was thinking about his mother and remembering the few times when he'd seen her smile. A tear appeared at the corner of his eye and rolled down his cheek. He thought killing Jameen would make him feel better, it didn't. Young didn't know how he felt about what they'd done. He dug into his pocket and pulled his phone out. Then he texted a message. Once he finished, he leaned sideways and drew his legs up. Then dozed off as they rode back to Augusta.

Noel was still up reading another urban novel when the text came through. He looked at the time, knowing that it was almost time to put his phone up. He set the book aside and sent a text to Kingston anyway. A Jamaican rule amongst bredren. Always show your appreciation for favors.

"Now if I could just get Alicia and this Jamaican Mafia under control," he mumbled.

"Huh, what was that Dredd?" His roommate asked. He was still asleep but must've overheard Noel mumble.

"Nothing man. Go back to sleep," Dredd told him.

His niece Alicia had always been hardheaded. He could remember when she was a little girl. She wouldn't listen to too many people. He knew that only a strong man could keep her in line. Right now, she was having her way down in Tampa Florida. Sheba had just told him that the FBI was investigating her crew for a number of murders. So, he had to do something about that.

This was why he was thinking of sending her to Augusta. Maybe D-Block and her sisters could keep her out of trouble. Or she'll meet herself a Thug, but she needed to be around some more *Lady Thugs*.

Noel reached over for the half of blunt he'd put out earlier. He fired it up and inhaled deeply. Yeah, his niece could use a change of scenery and he knew that she'd be at home in a *City Of Thugs!*

The End

Submission Guideline

Submit the first three chapters of your completed manuscript to ldpsubmissions@gmail.com, subject line: Your book's title. The manuscript must be in a .doc file and sent as an attachment. Document should be in Times New Roman, double spaced and in size 12 font. Also, provide your synopsis and full contact information. If sending multiple submissions, they must each be in a separate email.

Have a story but no way to send it electronically? You can still submit to LDP/Ca$h Presents. Send in the first three chapters, written or typed, of your completed manuscript to:

LDP: Submissions Dept
Po Box 944
Stockbridge, Ga 30281

DO NOT send original manuscript. Must be a duplicate.

Provide your synopsis and a cover letter containing your full contact information.

Thanks for considering LDP and Ca$h Presents.

<u>Coming Soon from Lock Down Publications/Ca\$h Presents</u>

BOW DOWN TO MY GANGSTA

By **Ca\$h**

TORN BETWEEN TWO

By **Coffee**

THE STREETS STAINED MY SOUL **II**

By **Marcellus Allen**

BLOOD OF A BOSS **VI**

SHADOWS OF THE GAME II

By **Askari**

LOYAL TO THE GAME **IV**

By **T.J. & Jelissa**

IF LOVING YOU IS WRONG… **III**

By **Jelissa**

TRUE SAVAGE **VIII**

MIDNIGHT CARTEL III

DOPE BOY MAGIC IV

CITY OF KINGZ II

By **Chris Green**

BLAST FOR ME **III**

A SAVAGE DOPEBOY III

CUTTHROAT MAFIA III

DUFFLE BAG CARTEL VI

By **Ghost**

A HUSTLER'S DECEIT III

KILL ZONE **II**

BAE BELONGS TO ME III

A DOPE BOY'S QUEEN III

By **Aryanna**

COKE KINGS V

KING OF THE TRAP II

By **T.J. Edwards**

GORILLAZ IN THE BAY V

3X KRAZY III

De'Kari

THE STREETS ARE CALLING II

Duquie Wilson

KINGPIN KILLAZ IV

STREET KINGS III

PAID IN BLOOD III

CARTEL KILLAZ IV

DOPE GODS III

Hood Rich

SINS OF A HUSTLA II

ASAD

KINGZ OF THE GAME VI

Playa Ray

SLAUGHTER GANG IV

RUTHLESS HEART IV

By Willie Slaughter

THE HEART OF A SAVAGE III

By Jibril Williams

FUK SHYT II

By Blakk Diamond

TRAP QUEEN

By Troublesome

YAYO V

GHOST MOB II

Stilloan Robinson

KINGPIN DREAMS III

By Paper Boi Rari

CREAM II

By Yolanda Moore

SON OF A DOPE FIEND III

By Renta

FOREVER GANGSTA II

GLOCKS ON SATIN SHEETS III

By Adrian Dulan

LOYALTY AIN'T PROMISED III

By Keith Williams

THE PRICE YOU PAY FOR LOVE II

By Destiny Skai

I'M NOTHING WITHOUT HIS LOVE II

SINS OF A THUG II

By Monet Dragun

LIFE OF A SAVAGE IV

MURDA SEASON IV

GANGLAND CARTEL III

CHI'RAQ GANGSTAS III

By **Romell Tukes**

QUIET MONEY IV

EXTENDED CLIP II

By **Trai'Quan**

THE STREETS MADE ME III

By **Larry D. Wright**

IF YOU CROSS ME ONCE II

ANGEL III

By **Anthony Fields**

FRIEND OR FOE III

By **Mimi**

SAVAGE STORMS III

By **Meesha**

BLOOD ON THE MONEY III

By J-Blunt

THE STREETS WILL NEVER CLOSE II

By K'ajji

NIGHTMARES OF A HUSTLA III

By King Dream

THE WIFEY I USED TO BE II

By Nicole Goosby

IN THE ARM OF HIS BOSS

By Jamila

MONEY, MURDER & MEMORIES II

Malik D. Rice

CONCRETE KILLAZ II

By Kingpen

HARD AND RUTHLESS II

By Von Wiley Hall

LEVELS TO THIS SHYT II

By Ah'Million

Available Now

RESTRAINING ORDER **I & II**

By **CA$H & Coffee**

LOVE KNOWS NO BOUNDARIES **I II & III**

By **Coffee**

RAISED AS A GOON I, II, III & IV

BRED BY THE SLUMS I, II, III

BLAST FOR ME I & II

ROTTEN TO THE CORE I II III

A BRONX TALE I, II, III

DUFFLE BAG CARTEL I II III IV V

HEARTLESS GOON I II III IV

A SAVAGE DOPEBOY I II

HEARTLESS GOON I II III

DRUG LORDS I II III

CUTTHROAT MAFIA I II

By **Ghost**

LAY IT DOWN **I & II**

LAST OF A DYING BREED I II

BLOOD STAINS OF A SHOTTA I & II III

By **Jamaica**

200

LOYAL TO THE GAME I II III

LIFE OF SIN I, II III

By **TJ & Jelissa**

BLOODY COMMAS I & II

SKI MASK CARTEL I II & III

KING OF NEW YORK I II,III IV V

RISE TO POWER I II III

COKE KINGS I II III IV

BORN HEARTLESS I II III IV

KING OF THE TRAP

By **T.J. Edwards**

IF LOVING HIM IS WRONG…I & II

LOVE ME EVEN WHEN IT HURTS I II III

By **Jelissa**

WHEN THE STREETS CLAP BACK I & II III

THE HEART OF A SAVAGE I II

By **Jibril Williams**

A DISTINGUISHED THUG STOLE MY HEART I II & III

LOVE SHOULDN'T HURT I II III IV

RENEGADE BOYS I II III IV

PAID IN KARMA I II III

SAVAGE STORMS I II

By **Meesha**

A GANGSTER'S CODE I &, II III

A GANGSTER'S SYN I II III

THE SAVAGE LIFE I II III

CHAINED TO THE STREETS I II III

BLOOD ON THE MONEY I II

By J-Blunt

PUSH IT TO THE LIMIT

By **Bre' Hayes**

BLOOD OF A BOSS **I, II, III, IV, V**

SHADOWS OF THE GAME

By **Askari**

THE STREETS BLEED MURDER **I, II & III**

THE HEART OF A GANGSTA I II& III

By **Jerry Jackson**

CUM FOR ME I II III IV V VI

An **LDP Erotica Collaboration**

BRIDE OF A HUSTLA **I II & II**

THE FETTI GIRLS **I, II& III**

CORRUPTED BY A GANGSTA I, II III, IV

BLINDED BY HIS LOVE

THE PRICE YOU PAY FOR LOVE

DOPE GIRL MAGIC I II III

By **Destiny Skai**

WHEN A GOOD GIRL GOES BAD

By **Adrienne**

THE COST OF LOYALTY I II III

By Kweli

A GANGSTER'S REVENGE **I II III & IV**

THE BOSS MAN'S DAUGHTERS I II III IV V

A SAVAGE LOVE **I & II**

BAE BELONGS TO ME I II

A HUSTLER'S DECEIT I, II, III
WHAT BAD BITCHES DO I, II, III
SOUL OF A MONSTER I II III
KILL ZONE
A DOPE BOY'S QUEEN I II
By **Aryanna**
A KINGPIN'S AMBITON
A KINGPIN'S AMBITION **II**
I MURDER FOR THE DOUGH
By **Ambitious**
TRUE SAVAGE I II III IV V VI VII
DOPE BOY MAGIC I, II, III
MIDNIGHT CARTEL I II
CITY OF KINGZ
By **Chris Green**
A DOPEBOY'S PRAYER
By **Eddie "Wolf" Lee**
THE KING CARTEL **I, II & III**
By **Frank Gresham**
THESE NIGGAS AIN'T LOYAL **I, II & III**
By **Nikki Tee**
GANGSTA SHYT **I II &III**
By **CATO**
THE ULTIMATE BETRAYAL
By **Phoenix**
BOSS'N UP **I , II & III**
By **Royal Nicole**

I LOVE YOU TO DEATH
By Destiny J
I RIDE FOR MY HITTA
I STILL RIDE FOR MY HITTA
By **Misty Holt**
LOVE & CHASIN' PAPER
By **Qay Crockett**
TO DIE IN VAIN
SINS OF A HUSTLA
By **ASAD**
BROOKLYN HUSTLAZ
By **Boogsy Morina**
BROOKLYN ON LOCK I & II
By **Sonovia**
GANGSTA CITY
By **Teddy Duke**
A DRUG KING AND HIS DIAMOND I & II III
A DOPEMAN'S RICHES
HER MAN, MINE'S TOO I, II
CASH MONEY HO'S
THE WIFEY I USED TO BE
By Nicole Goosby
TRAPHOUSE KING **I II & III**
KINGPIN KILLAZ I II III
STREET KINGS I II
PAID IN BLOOD **I II**
CARTEL KILLAZ I II III

DOPE GODS I II

By **Hood Rich**

LIPSTICK KILLAH **I, II, III**

CRIME OF PASSION I II & III

FRIEND OR FOE I II

By **Mimi**

STEADY MOBBN' **I, II, III**

THE STREETS STAINED MY SOUL

By **Marcellus Allen**

WHO SHOT YA **I, II, III**

SON OF A DOPE FIEND I II

Renta

GORILLAZ IN THE BAY **I II III IV**

TEARS OF A GANGSTA I II

3X KRAZY I II

DE'KARI

TRIGGADALE I II III

Elijah R. Freeman

GOD BLESS THE TRAPPERS I, II, III

THESE SCANDALOUS STREETS I, II, III

FEAR MY GANGSTA I, II, III IV, V

THESE STREETS DON'T LOVE NOBODY I, II

BURY ME A G I, II, III, IV, V

A GANGSTA'S EMPIRE I, II, III, IV

THE DOPEMAN'S BODYGAURD I II

THE REALEST KILLAZ I II III

Tranay Adams

THE STREETS ARE CALLING
Duquie Wilson
MARRIED TO A BOSS... I II III
By Destiny Skai & Chris Green
KINGZ OF THE GAME I II III IV V
Playa Ray
SLAUGHTER GANG I II III
RUTHLESS HEART I II III
By Willie Slaughter
FUK SHYT
By Blakk Diamond
DON'T F#CK WITH MY HEART I II
By Linnea
ADDICTED TO THE DRAMA I II III
IN THE ARM OF HIS BOSS II
By Jamila
YAYO I II III IV
A SHOOTER'S AMBITION I II
By S. Allen
TRAP GOD I II III
By Troublesome
FOREVER GANGSTA
GLOCKS ON SATIN SHEETS I II
By Adrian Dulan
TOE TAGZ I II III
LEVELS TO THIS SHYT
By Ah'Million

KINGPIN DREAMS I II

By Paper Boi Rari

CONFESSIONS OF A GANGSTA I II III

By Nicholas Lock

I'M NOTHING WITHOUT HIS LOVE

SINS OF A THUG

By Monet Dragun

CAUGHT UP IN THE LIFE I II III

By Robert Baptiste

NEW TO MONEY, MURDER & MEMORIES

THE GAME I II III

By **Malik D. Rice**

LIFE OF A SAVAGE I II III

A GANGSTA'S QUR'AN I II III

MURDA SEASON I II III

GANGLAND CARTEL I II

CHI'RAQ GANGSTAS I II

By **Romell Tukes**

LOYALTY AIN'T PROMISED I II

By Keith Williams

QUIET MONEY I II III

THUG LIFE I II

EXTENDED CLIP

By **Trai'Quan**

THE STREETS MADE ME I II

By **Larry D. Wright**

THE ULTIMATE SACRIFICE I, II, III, IV, V, VI

KHADIFI

IF YOU CROSS ME ONCE

ANGEL I II

By **Anthony Fields**

THE LIFE OF A HOOD STAR

By Ca$h & Rashia Wilson

THE STREETS WILL NEVER CLOSE

By K'ajji

CREAM

By Yolanda Moore

NIGHTMARES OF A HUSTLA I II

By King Dream

CONCRETE KILLAZ

By Kingpen

HARD AND RUTHLESS

By Von Wiley Hall

GHOST MOB II

Stilloan Robinson

BOOKS BY LDP'S CEO, CA$H

TRUST IN NO MAN

TRUST IN NO MAN 2

TRUST IN NO MAN 3

BONDED BY BLOOD

SHORTY GOT A THUG

THUGS CRY

THUGS CRY 2

THUGS CRY 3

TRUST NO BITCH

TRUST NO BITCH 2

TRUST NO BITCH 3

TIL MY CASKET DROPS

RESTRAINING ORDER

RESTRAINING ORDER 2

IN LOVE WITH A CONVICT

LIFE OF A HOOD STAR

CPSIA information can be obtained
at www.ICGtesting.com
Printed in the USA
BVHW062101250221
601128BV00015B/1564

9 781952 936876